The deadly roads and trails of life are markers that we want to keep in the rear-view mirror.

R CURTIS FORD

Jess

Enjoy the riches of Words!

R Curtis Ford

CONTENTS

Epigraph	
CHAPTER ONE	5
CHAPTER TWO	15
CHAPTER THREE	24
CHAPTER FOUR	37
CHAPTER FIVE	46
CHAPTER SIX	53
CHAPTER SEVEN	63
CHAPTER EIGHT	75
CHAPTER NINE	84
CHAPTER TEN	91
CHAPTER ELEVEN	100
CHAPTER TWELVE	109
CHAPTER THIRTEEN	118
CHAPTER FOURTEEN	130
CHAPTER FIFTEEN	139
CHAPTER SIXTEEN	148
CHAPTER SEVENTEEN	156
CHAPTER EIGHTEEN	165

CHAPTER NINETEEN	176
CHAPTER TWENTY	184
CHAPTER TWENTY-ONE	190
CHAPTER TWENTY-TWO	199
CHAPTER TWENTY-THREE	210
CHAPTER TWENTY-FOUR	218

Deadly Trails

Mysteries of a Detective #2

Deadly Trails

Mysteries of a Detective #2

R Curtis Ford

DEADLY TRAILS

Copyright © 2023 Robert C Ford

All rights reserved.

ISBN:979-8-9880465-0-9

DEDICATION

to
my wife, Ann, of over Sixty years
we are saying our Long Goodbye
and
my children who give my constant and loving support
Robert, Michael, and Andrea
pilgrims walking this journey together

CHAPTER ONE

He stumbled out the door of the doctor's office. Where is the car? Where did he park? It was the same place and town when he walked into the building. It was bright and sunny then. He almost fell into his car – a brand-new Corvette. It seemed like an old car now. He sat back in his car, trying not to shake so much. What did the doctor say?

I have Parkinson's? I have Parkinson's!

Roderick Carson, CEO and president of Carson Detective Agency, sat there for a while. His daily routine was to get breakfast with a lot of coffee and then drive to his office in Monterey, California.

"God, what are you doing? Life was humming along so well. Money was coming into the company, and it was flourishing. What do I do now? I'm feeling fine now," Rod said out loud."

His thoughts went to Cindy. Would she still want him as a boyfriend? What kind of future would she have with him?

Cindy Royston was a stunning girl Rod had met when her brother, Clint, was abducted. Cindy's father had contracted Rod and his Agency to find their son and brother. He had fallen for her initially, but he didn't act on his feelings until her brother was found alive and released.

Rod eventually started the car and drove slowly down the main street to his office. He forgot about getting his morning coffee at a nearby coffee shop. Soon Rod parked his car and just sat there. How was he going to tell Conrad and Sue?

Conrad Phillips was his right-hand detective, and Sue Stillard was hired by Rod's dad as a secretary even before Rod was salaried as a detective. What would happen to them?

Conrad could take the news. He is a challenging and rugged guy sporting many tattoos from his Navy days. A very casual dresser. Conrad had his Black Belt in Karate and loved to spar with anyone. He struggled with anger issues but learned to live with the past.

Sue had a very analytical mind and loved people. She lived in Monterey most of her life. Sue had blond-red hair and loved to fool people with her short-tempered reactions and teased just about everyone. Overall a kind and generous person.

Sue will probably take it hard. Oh well, it needs to be done.

Rod slowly exited the car and leaned against it for some time because he didn't know if his legs would take him up the stairs to the second-floor office.

Rod met Sue as he came in, so he said, "I need some time in my office, so if you brought in some coffee, I would appreciate it."

Sue gave him one of her memorable *what's going on* looks. But she said only, "Okay," and went to get him a cup. When she entered Rod's office, she said, "You want to talk about it?" Rod was looking out his favorite window, "Not now, give me some time, and when I'm ready, I'll call you and Conrad in." Sue turned and went out and closed his office door. She knew that when Rod was like this, agree, just give him some time. They were close colleagues, and she knew him well.

Rod was deep in thought when Conrad erupted into Rod's office.

"I've got some bad news. Jeff Marrone died this weekend. David received a call from one of his boys that he was found this morning. He missed a golf game yesterday morning, and when one of his golfing buddies didn't reach him by phone, he called the police for a welfare check. They found him in his easy chair. He might have had a heart attack. They don't know yet." Conrad said as he waited for a response.

The look on Rod's face was one Conrad had not seen before.

"Are you okay, Rod?"

After a moment, "Yes, I'm okay; I'm just trying to process this news. Was Jeff not feeling good? Did he have any heart problems? He never told me there were any health problems."

Conrad replied, "I don't think so. He never told David, either. David has not told anyone in our San Jose office yet. What do you think David should do?"

David Turner was Jeff's manager in the Marrone Detective Agency before they merged into the Carson Detective Agency.

"Go ahead and tell the people there. At some point, I will have to contact our attorneys about what happened to Jeff. Business-wise, I am not worried about it yet."

"David told me Jeff's boys are in awful shape this

morning. I mean, he was only sixty-four years old. David was heading to their home briefly after informing all the personnel there. He said he would let Jeff's kids know our thoughts and condolences."

"Let's drive up there a little later, and we can sit down and do some planning ourselves," Rod said with a heavy heart.

Rod sat back in his chair, reflected on this news, and once again realized the brevity of life. He then also thought about the disabling report he received this morning.

Less than two years ago, Rod first came in contact with Jeff. They met because Rod's detective agency needed to expand to handle two significant cases. Conrad, Rod's number one detective, had told him about the Marrone Detective Agency in San Jose and that they were in financial trouble. Soon after that, Rod met with Jeff and proposed a merger.

Everything from then on went fantastic. Jeff's death came right out of the blue.

Rod told Conrad, "If you don't mind, give me time to process this. Please close the door as you leave?"

Rod turned in his chair and stared out the big picture window. He always looked out when he needed to think. The scene outside the window showed part of the Cannery Row of Monterey and the beautiful bay.

He didn't see that scene now because his eyes were clouded over with tears. Rod never cried. Only when his mother died many years ago. Not like this. He cried because his business partner died, primarily because of the news he received this morning about his health. "God, how could you. This is too much." Rod said as he raised a fist toward the ceiling.

What came to Rod's mind was the Bible verse, *I won't leave you, and I will never abandon you.*

Rod dabbed his eyes with tissues he had on the small window side table. "Okay, God, I got your message," He said out loud.

Rod took a deep breath and headed for his office door. "Okay, guys, come in because I have other news for you."

Sue came in first and sat in the corner seating area. Conrad came in behind Sue and sat next to her on the settee. They both looked at Rod and saw the swelling around his eyes. Seeing this, Conrad was a little taken aback and said, "Boss, you're taking this hard. We can handle things around here for a while. Why don't you head home."

Sue picked up on the cue, "Yea, we've got it here; take some time off."

Rod came over and sat on the easy chair in front of both of them, "Yes, Jeff's death was so unexpected, but I have other news to give you," he took another drink of coffee, "Sue, remember last week when I stumbled as I went into my office?"

"Yes, I remember. You said you tripped on something."

"Well, that has happened several times lately. I've also had slight tremors; I'm a little slower than usual, sometimes not thinking right. So I made an appointment last week with my doctor. He checked me over and asked a lot of questions. He said I have Parkinson's."

Sue and Conrad looked at each other but could not speak.

Sue reacted faster than Conrad, "I'm so sorry, Rod. Then getting the news about Jeff. This all must seem overwhelming."

Conrad was deep in thought, "How do you feel now?"

He looked at Rod and said, "Listen, you know we will do anything to help you. You just have to let us know how. Let me drive to Northern California and meet with David and Jeff's boys."

Rod looked at them with tears, "You both mean so much to me. I'm perplexed about all this, but I need to keep busy. Conrad, I'm going with you, and maybe I can google about Parkinson's on the way up and learn what I can do to help myself."

"You think that's a good idea now?" Conrad said as he put his cup down. Rod leaned in closer. "Yes, I think it's the right thing to do. I don't feel that bad, so work is good medicine." Rod said but not believing what he said.

Conrad got up from the couch, "Okay, I'll call David and let him know we'll be on our way. Do you want this news about you to be kept quiet?"

"Let me think about that for a while. I'm heading home to get some clothes packed. How about picking me up at my place in about an hour."

Conrad said okay to Rod, "Sue, you got it here until we get back?"

"Sure, everything will be okay here. Are you sure you'll be okay going, Rod?"

"Yep, I'll be fine, Sue. I just need a road trip now. Pray for me as I meet with Jeff's boys and other family members. Also, I really would like your prayers because I will meet with Cindy. How can I tell her?"

Conrad spoke, "Straight forward, just like you do in other situations. I'll give you pointers on the way up."

They all laughed at that, but Rod had second thoughts deep down

The trip was quiet most of the way, with splashes of conversation intermixed with radio sounds. Conrad, for the first time, didn't know what to say. At times he made no sense at all. His thoughts were, *what can I say to make things better*. He also knew that that was impossible.

Finally, Rod sat up straighter and yawned. He asked Conrad, "How come you haven't said a word?"

"I have been you're just not listening to me. I'm sorry about the doctor's diagnosis and Jeff's passing, but we must let his boys know we are sorry for their loss."

"Isn't that what I said before we left?" Rod pointed out the front window, "That's our exit. Don't you know where we're going?"

Conrad laughed, "You have finally escaped that fog you were in. No, I didn't forget where we were going. Welcome back."

"I do feel better, physically and emotionally. If I have Parkinson's, I can do nothing about it right now." Rod said as he put on his shoes, "Are we going to the office first or to the Marrone home?"

"David said he would meet us at Jeff's place, so we're heading there first, then the office," Conrad said as he smiled when he took the exit.

Traffic was getting busier, so the conversation dimmed. It wasn't long before they arrived at Jeff's home just south of San Jose.

David met them when they pulled into the driveway. There were cars all over the place in the street. It seems that the word of Jeff's death went far and wide. Conrad and Rod were not surprised. "There are a lot of family and friends inside, and I told them they needed to be with family and friends now," David said as he turned to go inside, "We will be just a moment and then leave for the office."

Rod agreed with David, and they went inside. The size of the group *did* surprise them. David introduced Conrad and Rod to Jason and Ryan, Jeff's boys. They really looked like him. Ryan was taking it the hardest. Ryan was the youngest of the two boys. He recently got his CPA license and worked at a large company in Berkeley. Ryan was somewhat shy. He was astute, but his one major problem was his quick temper.

Rod expressed his sincere condolences to them. "We are very sorry for your loss, and your family and friends are here to grieve with you. I'm sure that's good to see. We won't be long; if there is anything we can do for you, just let us know. David will let us know when the arrangements are put together."

Jason responded, "Thank you very much for stopping by now. It means a lot to us. We can sure tell that Dad was loved and appreciated. I know there will be some business that needs to be done at the right time."

Jason Marrone is a self-assured man. He worked as a Real Estate person in the San Francisco area.

As they returned to the car, Rod said, "I think it's a good idea we get over to the office in San Jose to meet with David and encourage him and the staff.

Rod took out his cell phone, "Sue, we made it just fine. Yes, I'm doing better. If you can, I would like you to check the files about our merger and what it says about the death of one of the partners. I think I remember, but I need to know for sure. Also, we have to sign a new contract concerning the Carson Detective Agency. At some point, I need to find out what Jeff's arrangement was about the building he owned where our agency is in that building." Rod then put his phone away in his shirt pocket.

Rod was heavy in thought to God. *Again, you have challenged me to think of you more often and realize that life is short. Why do we wait to think about death until it's too late? Help me today to gather my thoughts and also help me to be a comfort to others.*

When they arrived at their San Jose office, Rod checked the voice messages from the weekend. Several were inquiries about divorce investigations, and one was about a child custody dispute. He finally listened to the last one from an old family friend, a business lawyer, Joseph Brooks. He only said he needed help quick and gave Rod his cell phone number. He sounded really anxious, and for that reason, Rod called right away.

"Hello Joe, we haven't spoken in years. What can I do to help?"

Joseph's voice was unsteady: "Hi, Rod; I knew you would get back to me quickly. Do you remember my son, Roger?"

"Yes, but it has been a long time since I've seen him. Maybe ten or twelve years."

"I think he went on a one-week hike in Kings Canyon National Park; at least, that's what he told us. That was three weeks ago. No one has heard from him since. We've been frantic, and Dawn, Angel, and I have called and texted many times with no response. His friends said he had just disappeared. We called the police, and all they did was issue a missing person's report."

"Rod said, "Have they got anywhere with that report."

"Only they contacted the area's law enforcement and the Kings Canyon National Park authorities."

"Let me start digging. Do you still live in the Napa Valley area?" As he jotted down what Joe had told him,

Rod said, "Send me as much material about Roger that you think would help me start the investigation. Starting with age, height, weight, and acquaintances."

"I'll do that right away. Please find our son. If you need any money now, please let me know."

"Don't worry about money now. I'll get right on it. Oh, and send me your and Roger's contact information. Also, send me some latest pictures of Roger. Call if anything new happens, like if he calls anytime. Bye."

Rod pushed back from his desk. *What else can go wrong? Here we go again.*

CHAPTER TWO

People started to come to the office to convey their condolences. The response again showed Rod and Conrad that Jeff was well-liked in the community.

There was a table set up for refreshments. Jordan Chavez, the Agency receptionist, and Victoria Weaver, the Administrative Assistant, were chatting with those who came in and ensuring they had some appetizers.

Rod notified the staff there would be a meeting at nine the following day. A lot was going on now, so today would be impossible to meet with the workforce.

Rod cornered Conor and David, "Can we meet in my office upstairs to review some concerns." Rod told Jordan about their meeting upstairs, "I don't think it will be too long. We will get back downstairs as soon as we can."

"How are you doing, David?" Rod said, "You've known Jeff the longest, and I'm sure this is hard for you. Is it okay if we continue with a short meeting?" Rod said as he looked at a sad fellow worker. "No, I'm okay. It was such a shock. I think working is the best remedy for me now. Let's go ahead." David responded with an understandable, heavy heart.

Rod sat back and looked at them, "I will contact our

lawyer here and find out the next steps. I seem to remember that our contract has provisions for instances like this. I also think it's time to add more staff, maybe two more detectives and another administrative person. We are growing, and we need help. We now have enough administrative support, but I'm thinking about Sue. She and Aaron are getting along well, and I don't think it will be long before he pops *the* question."

Sue Stillard was Rod's dad's secretary with the original Carson Detective Agency. Sue was divorced with two children. Her mom also lived in the area. While Sue was working, her mom and another woman took turns caring for her son, Josh, and daughter, Jill. With Sue spending more time with Aaron, they all agreed that the kids would stay with Sue's mom. Aaron helped with the cost, so her mom wouldn't have to work outside her home.

Conrad was surprised by what Rod said about Sue, "I guess I'm about as clueless as you are, sometimes, Rod. I didn't see that one coming. Okay, it makes sense now to add another admin assistant in Monterey. I think David and I agree about hiring a few more detectives."

Rod leaned forward, "I would like you both to work on the hiring. Also, I told Conrad in my office that we have a new case, and I want you guys to work on that. It will be the *Brooks* case. Joe Brooks is a friend of my family and his son Roger is missing. Conrad, you can fill David in on the specifics at the right time. I will briefly set out to the Brooks home to gather more information."

"David, keep us advised about the arraignments for Jeff's funeral. Also, you can let Conrad know if you need time to get away." Rod said as his hands began to shake. "There is something else to tell you. I know this may not be the best time, but we all know it's never the best time for things to happen. David, I was diagnosed this morning with Parkinson's."

David's eyes dropped to the floor, "I don't know what to say. I'm sorry, Rod."

"There's nothing you can do but pray. Pray that I'll be strong enough to do my job and be able to support those who are grieving, and in the Brooks case, I want to help them because they are old friends of my family."

David looked at Conrad, then Rod, "You know, Rod, we will step up to the plate and deliver whatever needs to be done."

"I know that David. I want you and Conrad to continue our business and support our staff. They are hurting." Rod replied, "Don't tell the staff yet about my diagnosis. I'll tell them at the right time, probably after Jeff's funeral. Okay, let's cheer up a little at least and be a comfort to those who are downstairs."

They stood then, and Conrad said, "Rod, I know David well enough to tell you that we support you and will walk you down this uncertain trail."

It didn't take long to get to Joe Brook's home. Rod was eager to meet them again, but not under these circumstances. It had been at least twelve years since he had last seen them. Rod's dad was a friend of Joe Brooks since they were in college together. Joe had set up the original contract for the Carson Detective Agency.

Rod was met at the door by Joe's wife, Dawn. "Come on in, Rod, it has been a long time. How are you doing?" She said as they walked to Joe's office. Joe came around the desk and gave Rod a big hug. "You look terrific. You've been working out, haven't you?"

"No, it's just the way my jacket fits. Makes me look more buff." Rod responded as he took his jacket off. "Where's Angel? I'm sure she has greatly changed since I last saw her."

Dawn responded, "She's changed a lot. She is married now, and they have our first grandchild. I don't think you would recognize her."

Rod sat back on the office chair, "My goodness, it has been a long time."

"I can't stay long this time, so we better get down to business. Start at the beginning and tell me the story about Roger. You know, the who, what, where, and why of his disappearance."

As Joe and Dawn discussed their son, they had difficulty grasping why he went missing. The story seemed normal. It would be tough to get to the truth, no matter how hard it might be. They exchanged contact information and gave Rod up-to-date pictures of Roger. Rod began to consider that this case might be long and difficult.

"I think that is about all I can get now. I have assigned two of the best detectives to the case. I also will be heavily involved. Conrad Phillips and David Turner will be following up with you. Thank you for your time, and you know we will work very hard to bring your son home." As Rod finished, Joe's wife broke down. "I know you will. Bring him home safe."

As Rod left, he had another one of those premonitions deep down in his gut that something was really wrong. He also knew that you should rely on something other than hunches.

When Rod returned to the office, he found Conrad hard at work on the phone with what Rod thought was a candidate for one of the detective positions. Rod sat down and waited for him to get off the phone. Conrad indicated by his trigger finger in the air Rod took just a minute.

Conrad said goodbye and then looked up at Rod with a big smile. "I'm sure that one will be one of our new detectives. Her name is Jada Davis. She has great abilities and was spoken highly of by her past employer at the LAPD. One of her specialties is in the computer field. I've also received a great lead from a colleague at the Phoenix PD. My friend talked about a guy named Joshua Helms. He worked in Homicide there for twelve years and wants to move to this area to be closer to his ailing parents."

"You've been busy," Rod said as he moved closer to Conrad's desk. "By the way, where's David?"

"I sent him back over to the Marrone home. He was not himself, and I told him I had some leads and could handle whatever went on at the office. I hope you don't mind. I told David not to come back until after the funeral. He thanked me, said he was not thinking right, and agreed."

"Of course, I don't mind. You're becoming a first-class executive. I mean that."

Rod was pleased with Conrad and has shown extraordinary managerial abilities, especially since the merger. "You've been a great help to me today. I'm beginning to understand that I may need more help."

"I appreciate that, Rod. I know we will miss Jeff, but things are happening fast around here, and I always feel more at ease." Conrad said as he put his pen down and leaned back.

Rod sipped his coffee, "I told Joe Brooks that you and David will be the lead in that case. We should call the local law enforcement where he said he was going. Also, we need to contact the Kings Canyon Park rangers and get them involved if they're not already."

Conrad had that satisfied look on his face, "I already called the Fresno Police Department, the Fresno County Sheriff's Department, and the Sequoia National Forest Rangers about Roger Brooks."

Rod laughed and stood, "See, you don't need me at all."

Conrad laughed, "Oh, come on, I know who the big Boss is, and I'll never forget that you run this place. Something is going on there in the mountains. Both agencies told me there are more missing people than Roger Brooks on a hiking trail called the Rae Lakes Loop near Cedar Grove, California. This could be a lot bigger than a missing persons case. David is excited for us to get over there as soon as possible after the funeral."

"Great work," Rod said.

"Rod, there is something I'm going to tell you, and I don't want any argument. I'm not going with David to Fresno and Kings Canyon Park. I feel deeply that I should stay and be in charge around here for a while until we see how you're doing. There is enough going on that would be hard for a person dealing with a partner's death; besides, Cindy needs you now, and you need her." Conrad saw that Rod was about to say something, "I said I'm staying here. No disagreement."

Rod turned as he got to the door, "Okay, Conrad, I know when I'm beaten. Thanks, good friend. I'm heading over to Cindy Royston's place for some relaxation. I want to see how her family is doing. I called Cindy on the way here, and she's happy I'm coming. I think I'll stay overnight there – they have numerous bedrooms, and her dad, Clinton Royston, said I could stay anytime. I don't know how she is going to take my diagnosis. Let me know of any new developments on the Brooks case or anything else significant."

Rod was ready to get away for a while. He snatched some different clothes in his office and was soon in his Corvette for the hour-plus drive. Rod jumped on the toll road because the other way through San Francisco was almost an hour and a half long, and this way was much quieter and straighter. It was such a beautiful summer day he decided to put the top down before he left San Jose.

He cranked up the radio and sang along with the contemporary gospel music he enjoyed. He did not care when other drivers laughed at him. He was ready to see Cindy. But how was she going to take the news?

He finally turned down the radio as he approached the Royston estate. He saw Cindy sitting with her brother Clint Jr. Clint was involved in a kidnapping case Rod had a few years before. He had spent some time in federal prison but not very long. Rod thought the authorities let him go early because Clint's dad was the Assistant Secretary of State for the U.S. government. Rod realized that Cindy and her brother had grown very close together after the dust had settled from that case.

As Cindy saw Rod's Corvette turn in their driveway, she jumped up and ran to meet him. She hugged him because it had been some time since she had seen him. "Hi, good looking," she said as he let her down on her feet. "It's been way too long. I hope you won't say hi and leave. Are you leaving?"

"No, not this time. You get me until tomorrow or even longer. I have a couple of things to tell you, though. Jeff

Marrone passed away this past weekend. I don't know when the funeral will be, so I may have to return earlier."

"Okay, sorry to hear about Jeff. Was he sick?"

"No, not that any of us heard or seen. Jeff died in his easy chair. He might have had a massive heart attack."

"Oh," she paused to look into his eyes, "What is the other thing?"

"Let's go find a quiet room so we can talk," Rod said as he took her arm to lead her into the house.

"Okay, you're scaring me now."

They went into the den and sat down on the sofa.

"Cindy, what I'm about to tell you is not easy."

"Oh, come on, out with it."

"Okay, earlier this morning, I had an appointment with my doctor. I have been having some issues with balance, not thinking right, some tremors, so I decided to see what it might be," Rod could not look at her, "I have Parkinson's."

Cindy started crying, and Rod got his handkerchief and gave it to her.

She threw her arms around him, "I'm so sorry, Rod. I wish I could have been with you during this. What can I do?"

"All I know to do is love and don't leave me."

"Leave you? What are you talking about? Don't you know I'm in love with you? I would never leave you."

They sat there for some time, talking and talking and holding hands. Sometimes it was just better to be quiet.

Finally, Rod stood up and pulled her up, "I want our time together to be very special and Memorable."

"What do you mean by that, *memorable*?" Cindy said, tilting her head to the side with a questioning look.

"What I mean is, I'm yours until at least tomorrow.

Rod again pondered what the future would be like.

CHAPTER THREE

The *Celebration of Life* for Jeff Marrone was the following Saturday. Because many wanted to attend the service, Jason and Ryan Marrone decided to have it in their large church. Rod was beginning to find out that Jeff's life reached numerous people from different backgrounds and abilities. Rod thought, *Why do we find out what a person is like at their funeral. The questions that enter our mind. I didn't know that about them?*

Aaron Sterling picked up Sue and headed north the day before the service. Rod and Conrad traveled up the coast to be with the rest of the staff of the Carson Detective Agency.

Aaron was the owner and CEO of Sterling, Inc., located in Los Angeles, California. His company's CFO was involved in one of the largest embezzlements in the country. Aaron's youngest son, William, was also involved in the embezzlement and is now in prison.

It, indeed, was a *Celebration of Life*. Jason and Ryan gave their dad a moving tribute to his life. Ryan needed help finishing his talk. The minister obviously knew Jeff because he referenced their times together as a minister and friend.

Looking around at his staff, Rod could tell that many, especially those who worked with Jeff in San Jose, were moved to tears. It was a colossal loss to them.

The service was short, and the gravesite was only for family members.

The staff decided to go to a local restaurant for a late lunch. David told the group about his personal relationship with Jeff, which was both serious and funny. He ended his talk with, "Memories are the gifts God gives us to honor our friends. Collect the good recollections."

This side of David, Rod had never seen before. Death can bring out a more tender component of our personality

Aaron took Rod aside and told him he would take Sue away for a few days. Rod replied, "That's great. She needs some time away because she will be busy returning to Monterey. With that said, Aaron strode away with a bounce in his steps. All Rod could do was watch as Aaron told Sue they were going out for a few days. This brought a smile to Rod's face. He then thought of Cindy and wondered if this would be a good time for them to escape. Rod also considered his illness and how much time he would have on earth.

Conrad came over with a severe look. Conrad took Rod to a quieter corner of the restaurant.

"I just received a call from a Ranger Station at the Kings Canyon National Park. They found a body on that hiking trail I told you about. By what they said of the description, it's not Roger. They think it's one of the other three missing persons. They said it looked like a homicide but would have to wait for the coroner's report. The Fresno Sheriff's Dept. is coming to the location."

Rod thought briefly, "David and that new guy you hired

need to take a trip to the park; maybe it will be extended. What was his name, Joshua?"

"Okay, I'll call him right away. He's already moved here, and I'm sure he is anxious to start. I will plan on them leaving Monday morning sometime."

"Sounds good to me, I'm heading up with Cindy to her home, and I'll be at the office Monday morning. Cindy took the news about my disease better than I thought she would." Rod said.

Rod went over to where Cindy was seated, "Hi, again; I've some good and some not-so-good news. I was going to spend a few days with you to get away, but something happened in a new case that involved a friend of my family. I can take you to your home, but I have to be back at the San Jose office Monday morning."

"Is this one of those times that having a Detective Agency where you have to drop everything and leave?" Cindy said with a cute little smile. "Yep, you're right again. I remembered that conversation a year or so ago. I was apprehensive that you would never want to see me again." They both laughed, remembering Rod's expression back then.

Monday morning came way too early for Rod and Cindy. They had a short-term but wonderful time just hanging out together. They talked about Rod's Parkinson's and how he was feeling. Cindy's family knew some very good Neurologists in San Francisco. She suggested Rod needed a second opinion on his diagnosis. "Dad knows this doctor well and can set up an appointment if that's okay with you."

"Sure, that's a great idea. I've been thinking about that

also. I appreciate you and your family's kindness."

But even good things must come to an end. They said their goodbyes, and Cindy reached up and kissed Rod this time. "*Now*," she said, "*I* can be just as aggressive as you, Rod."

Rod stood momentarily, catching his breath, "I love you, Cindy. I can't wait until the next time. How about you plan something for us the next time." Cindy returned with a quick, "How about we go to a bridal shop," She said as she turned and ran to the house. As she turned again by the door to go in, Rod was still standing in the same place, looking after her.

For Rod, Monday came way too fast. It was another rainy day, but even the rain couldn't diminish his spirits.

When Rod arrived at the San Jose office, David placed gear in his car. "Ah, good, I made it in time. I thought that I might have missed you guys. Joshua is going with you, isn't he?" Rod said as he came over to David's new car. "How do you like your new car? That older car was getting beat up."

David answered as he closed the trunk lid. "I really like this one. It has all the bells and whistles. It even tells me when a cop is around."

Joshua came out and put some items in the back seat. Rod approached him with an extended hand, "Hello, my name is Rod. Welcome to the firm. I hope we're not rushing you."

Joshua gave Rod a big hug and then stood back. "David called me at the right time. I was filling out some resumés but don't need them now. I can't wait to get started. Conrad and David told me that the missing person's family is an old friend of yours. What are they like?"

"Good people, their boy, Roger, I didn't know him very well. The last time I saw him was when he was a teenager. I'll go over to their home, give them an update, and try to get more information about him while I'm there." Rod continued, "Come in for a minute to my office because I want to learn more about you. Also, David, if you need any arrangements for the trip, let me know."

David replied, "I already let Jordan know all that info, and if there are any changes or updates, I'll let her know. You can call anytime, though."

Aaron and Sue drove back to Monterey to let Sue off at her office, where she left her car.

Aaron said as they entered the office, "Sue, I had a wonderful time at the resort with you. As you can tell, I want to see you more often. I need to get back home and then to my office. There is so much to do. I need to hire some executives because it's too much work for me alone."

Sue kissed him, "I'll be waiting for your phone call. Make it soon."

Aaron left, but his thoughts were divided. A lot on Sue and some on his business. He knew he was in love with Sue, but did she feel the same? *Oh well, I'll work on that later.*

Since his CFO embezzled tons of money and was killed, he needed to get a new CFO soon. He had all the feelers out, but there could be some news when he returned to his office. What hurt him the most was his son's imprisonment because he was implicated in the embezzlement.

Aaron also wanted to get someone to prepare for CEO or Executive Vice President. Business went on, and Aaron needed people that were well-vetted and competent in upper management

Rod called Joe Brooks and asked if he could come over.

Joe met Rod outside when Rod pulled into the driveway. "I want to catch you outside because I don't want Dawn to hear." As they leaned against Rod's car, Joe said, "I found out a couple of things about Roger that you need to know," Joe took a deep breath, "I contacted Roger's girlfriend and asked her some questions. She told me that Roger had some problems with drugs and alcohol. His girlfriend also told me he owed money to a guy he knew. She didn't know his name, but by what Roger said, that guy was a bad man. What do you think, Rod? Could this be why he went missing?"

"I don't know, Joe, it could be or maybe not." Rod said as he thought about it, "Anything is possible. I've got two of my best detectives on their way to Kings Canyon National Park. These guys are good, and I'm sure they will come up with something. Joe, this could be a long case, so be prepared. If you don't hear from me, that doesn't mean we haven't been working on the subject, or it's terrible news. Is there anything else that would help?

"No, that's all. Find my boy and bring him back safely. I wanted to let you know what Roger's girlfriend said. It may or may not be true."

"You know, Joe, we will give it our best."

David and Josh's trip to Fresno was mostly guy talk, sports, guns, and family life. Both were married with children, so they spent much time talking about their kids. David had been around police most of his life and found their conversation compatible. He learned a lot about Josh's life and character.

After what seemed like a long time, they pulled into the hotel they were checking in at after the long drive from San Jose. "Josh, get a good sleep tonight, and we can meet at the hotel cafeteria for breakfast at 6:30. I feel it will be a long day tomorrow."

In San Jose, at their offices, Rod and Conrad were busy with some new minor cases and catching up with voice communications and notes from staff about Jeff's funeral. The employees seemed dejected at first, but they got down to business after a while.

Conrad came into Rod's office and sat down, "Good morning; I just received a call from a friend of mine, Juan, a detective with the Fresno Police Department. He told me two people who co-owned a Fitness Club in Fresno were missing this morning. Juan knew some Sheriff Deputies that told him the Fitness Club was locked up this morning. He also said their landlord said they had not returned from their weekend hike in Kings Canyon National Park. What's going on there?"

"That's good information, Conrad; call David and inform him of this new information. It may be related; who knows?"

"By the way, boss, tell me more about how Cindy took the news about your Parkinson's? How have you been feeling?"

"You know Cindy, she cried but was very supportive," Rod said as he put down his soft drink, "I did have some problems there, you know, tremors, slow to think sometimes. There was something else. Cindy's dad is contacting a Neurologist for me to have a second opinion."

Rod took another drink, "I hate to admit it. Still, as I was driving here, I hit a curb. Fortunately, there were no cars around. That bothered me a lot. I've been reading about Parkinson's and Conrad. I think it's time for me to let others do the driving. If I'm feeling good, I can make short trips but no longer ones; I'm afraid I might hurt others."

Conrad put down his coffee cup, "I think that's a wise decision. Also, I agree with you; it's time to tell the staff here. How about I set up a staff meeting for one this afternoon. Then we all can help when needed."

"Okay, you're right. The staff does need to know what's going on with me. Thanks for your help."

Rod, for some reason, was very uneasy as he entered the large conference room that afternoon, "I want to thank each of you for coming today. I also want to thank you for your response to Jeff's passing. Some of you have been here for a long time, and this unexpected death caused us to consider our own lives and how we can improve and be better people."

Rod took a deep breath, "I have had a series of mishaps that led me to go to my doctor last Monday morning. After checking me out and asking many questions, he told me I had Parkinson's. I'm feeling good right now, but this affects my thinking; my hands shake, and sometimes my vision is not so good. I also want you to know that I will see a Neurologist soon for a second opinion."

Rod continued as he looked around the room, "With that said, I told Conrad this morning I will be here and stay here as long as I can if it turns out to be, in fact, Parkinson's disease. The unfortunate part is that I have to park my Corvette," Rod paused, "No, none of you can have it." They all laughed and then got serious.

Rod went on, "All of you mean so much to me, and I know that you will continue on whether I'm here or not. We will miss Jeff a whole bunch and his personality. I will miss our talks and times together. Okay, do you have any questions?"

Of course, Sandi raised her hand. Sandra Bradley was the Administrative Head of the old Marrone Detective Agency. She was Headstrong and was used to having her own way.

"Yes, Sandi?" Rod said.

"I think I can speak for everyone. We are deeply sorry and saddened to hear about your diagnosis. As you know, when you first arrived on the scene, I was not a happy camper," The staff all laughed, including Sandi, "But now, because of Jeff's death, I am so grateful that you are our boss. You have shown us what a place should be run like, but you have been extraordinarily kind and generous to each one. Thank you, Rod, for your honesty and commitment to this Agency.

Everyone stood and clapped and cheered. There were also tears.

Rod wiped away what he thought was dust in the air, "I can't thank you enough, Sandi, for what you said and your reaction. While you are here, I want Conrad to fill you in on our new case or cases. We have a lot of work to do, so after he's done, you are dismissed so we can get some work done."

Conrad took the next 20 minutes explaining what he knew and the case's implications. A few questions were asked and answered. It was a somber group that left the meeting.

The Rae Lakes Loop panorama was both rugged and absolutely gorgeous. One moment you are struggling up a switchback, and out of breath, you crest a rise, and before you, a scene straight out of a National Park magazine. Trails that stretch out for miles only to take you to another switchback. Some patches of snow will be at six to eleven thousand feet, even in late summer.

The numerous lakes are crystal clear, with trout and other creatures enjoying unlimited food. Signs of bears and other animals dot the landscape. At higher elevations, the marmots, giant-type squirrels, scurry around, always looking for food.

Unfortunately, some people who hike need to be more careful about what they do with their trash. These same people try to feed every animal they see, unaware that animals can fend for themselves. It also brings more animals to the trail expecting a dinner. Those who know what they're doing will only stop this practice if they see the outcome. More people will get hurt if that practice is continued.

Park Rangers try to put bear-proof containers for litter and bear-proof containers to shelter food at campsites in convenient spots.

One of the couples who did not care about the scenery because of their unhealthy habits was Derik Thomson and Elizabeth Fox from the Fresno, California, area. Both had a drug addiction, especially Derik. He and Beth were friends mainly because Beth was a cling-on. She thought she loved Derik and would do almost anything if Derik asked her to. Despite his drug habit, Derik was fit to hike like this one. He had heard about the Rae Loop and decided to get away and do some hiking. He took Beth along for kicks, and she would be company on cold nights in a tent.

When they arrived at Dollar Lake, they planned to camp there for a few days.

The morning of the second day there, Derik saw another couple. He recognized the guy right away. He was Al Fletcher, but Derik did not identify the girl with him. Derik had known Al in Derik's teenage years as a guy that used to do drugs but now owned a Fitness Club.

Al was acquainted with many drug users and tried to get them to stop. He had crossed paths with Derik, and the outcome was not good. Derik thought Al was a phony and didn't like what he said about drugs. Derik knew better. He was more intelligent than Al. Derik enjoyed his lifestyle. He also had a lot of shadowy friends.

Something boiled up in Derik. He would avoid Al for now, at least for now. He would wait until another time.

David contacted their law enforcement partners in the area. He agreed to meet them at the Trailhead of the Rae Lake Loop in Kings Canyon National Park.

Besides Roger Brooks missing, David realized from Conrad that two more people were also missing.

David and Josh drove through Cedar Grove, California, to get to what the locals call *Roads End*. Cedar Grove has one of the Visitor Centers for the Sequoia and Kings Canyon National Parks.

When they pulled into the parking area, they saw a lot of Law Enforcement vehicles, plus many cars, trucks, and vans that they felt belonged to hikers. This was a favorite location to trek because it was the famous Pacific Crest Trail and John Muir Trail. Most of the trails in the area were considered moderately complex to very hard. As Josh started to get out of the car, he said, "Dave, this is not going to be easy. Look at those mountains."

"Well, we're young; we can handle anything, right?" David responded as he also took in the scenery.

They walked over to a group of sheriff deputies and introduced themselves. "We're from the Carson Detective Agency, and we need to speak to the person in charge, Josh said.

They were directed to the Sheriff of Fresno County.

After introducing themselves to the Sheriff, and told him they were contracted by Roger Brook's dad to search for him. The Sheriff welcomed them and told them about what had been done so far. "We have the Park Rangers here, so let's get together with their Lead Ranger. I think we have some news for you."

"As you may or may not know, we now have at least three missing persons. We did find one body so far that the Rangers brought down from the mountains," the sheriff went on, "With the picture and description we received from San Jose of Roger Brooks, the body is male but not his body.

The two people we know are missing are Becky Savage, age 30, of Fresno, and her co-owner of the Fresno Fitness Club, Al Fletcher, age 31, also of Fresno. We believe the body is possibly Al Fletcher, but it was hard to identify because of the shape the body was in when we found it. We have a good idea that Becky is still up there somewhere."

In the following thirty minutes, the team reviewed what had been completed. With some maps, they described where the body was found and the general area. To both David and Josh, they were in for some challenging hiking.

Fortunately, it was later in the summer, so most of the snow was gone except at the higher elevations.

The Lead Park Ranger described the body's location and what would happen next: "We will be searching in a search pattern that takes us up along the Rae Lakes Loop. Fortunately, the bridge we have to cross the King's River is new, so we can make a better time that way. Once we cross that bridge, we will be in units of four law enforcement officers. If anyone has problems with high altitude, please excuse yourself because this will be an arduous hike. Let me warn you to carry something more than a 9mm with you because bears are getting hungry this time of year," the Ranger said with a big smile, "okay, everyone, I'm not joking!"

Several sheriff's deputies decided they were not fit for this action. What was left was five groups of four people. Two radios were given to each group, and the Lead Ranger went around to each group to introduce himself and to get personal information from each person.

Dave and Josh had brought hiking equipment and gear they would need, knowing there would be some strenuous hiking. So with a backpack packed and heavy weapons, they headed over to the other two people.

After finding out more about their partners, they filled their water containers for the start of the hike.

Josh tapped Dave on his shoulder, "What did you get me into? Is this part of the detective business?

CHAPTER FOUR

Aaron was at his office by nine-thirty Tuesday morning going over his emails and snail-mail when his secretary entered, "Good morning, Mr. Sterling, how about a nice hot cup of coffee."

"That will be great. How have things been around here? I bet it's been hectic," Aaron said as he threw some notes and mail in the trash, "If you have a moment a little later, please come in so we can discuss where we stand on hiring some executives."

Aaron had contacted one of the most favorite Executive search firms in America. Unfortunately, he did not use this firm when he hired his last CFO, who took a lot of money from his firm. This time it will be different.

As Aaron was checking his business phone messages, there were a couple of calls from that firm. Aaron was taking the information down when his secretary came in and sat by his desk. Aaron had hired Ann Summons many years ago. She was the best private secretary and office manager he had ever seen.

After he finished and put the phone down, he turned to her, "I have received several great prospects for the CFO position and a few for the CEO. I'm going to be really careful, so here are the names of the candidates. Call the Carson Detective Agency to hire them to do background checks. I want them to take their time on these, and also, I want them to give me their best two or three persons that we can interview."

"Just to let you know, Mr. Sterling, we did extensive cleaning and remodeling of the CFO's offices. Also, some good prospects came in for the VP of Domestic Operations."

Aaron had a good day working because he wanted to catch up on all the items that had been neglected. Aaron also wanted to put on paper what had happened two years ago and what he needed to do to make sufficient changes.

Ann asked if he needed anything else, "No thanks, Ann; would you please contact my driver. I'll be leaving in about an hour from now." Aaron said as he got back to work.

Conrad picked up Rod at seven and went to breakfast in San Jose.

After the food was delivered, Conrad cleared his throat. "Ah, boss, *ahaaa*," "Come on, Conrad, out with it. What's going on?"

"I'm sorry. I don't know whether I should share this with you."

"Conrad, we've been friends for a long time, and just because I have Parkinson's, doesn't mean I can't handle what you've got to say. I feel you will know when I cannot receive bad news."

"You're right again," as he took a bite of his eggs, "We may have some issues at the office. Eva and Sandra had a big shouting match yesterday after we left. Jordan called me last night and told me. Do you want me to handle it?"

Yolanda (Eva) Ramirez was a detective at the Marrone

Agency before Rod was on the scene. She was a friend of Sandi's, but Eva began to see what Sandi was really like.

Rod responded, "No, let's see what the temperature is at the office when we get there. I won't let something like this go on."

"On another note, I heard from David later last night. They are heading up to the mountains early today. They have five teams of four people each for the search. David also said that the Sheriff of Fresno County recognized Josh from some conference they attended a few years ago. I think we hired a good man as a detective."

"Where did you go last night?" Elizabeth said with a pouty lip.

"Don't worry about it. I just took a little walk," Derik said with a snarl, "You bug me too much. Just leave me alone."

"Did you hear that noise down by the lake last night?"

"Listen, will you? Just shut up. I said don't worry about it."

Derik lost his cool and backhanded her across the face.

"Why do you hit me like that? I love you and will do anything you ask." She said, "Please don't hit me like that."

"You'll get more than that if you don't shut up," Derik replied angrily as he walked away. "I'm going down to the lake, but you stay here. I've got something to do down there."

"Take me with you," Elizabeth pleaded.

Derik turned to her with a look that scared her, and she started to back away.

Too late, Derik was on her like a lion in the wild. She

didn't have time to scream. He took out his knife and held it at her throat. He pulled the knife back, and very quietly, Derik whispered, "I told you to keep still and stay here. I will not take any more lip from you."

Elizabeth lay there for a few minutes, then stood and turned away from Derik. He did not see the stark panic on her face. How was she going to get away from him? Elizabeth didn't even know where she was. She followed him without looking where she was or how to return to the trailhead.

Derik stood by a nearby cliff, contemplating what his next move was. He turned to Elizabeth and shouted, "This is your last warning. I could get rid of you. No one would ever know."

Local police and sheriff department officers had been stationed at Roads End and the other trailhead of the Rae Lakes Loop Trail. They spoke to and searched every person leaving the area because of the murder victim found by the Rangers a few days before.

The search teams that were organized started their hike up the trail. David, Josh, and the other two men on their team were going along at a good pace because, at this lower level, there was not much climbing. They knew that wouldn't last long because the strenuous hiking was coming up.

The two groups up front were mostly Park Rangers and were already looking for anything suspicious along the trail. They knew the body was recovered near Dollar Lake, so they didn't want to make any mistakes.

It was almost twenty miles from Roads End to Dollar Lake, with an elevation of about ten thousand feet.

Fortunately, the National Park Rangers and workers had developed this trail into a first-class hiking experience. The path usually offered space for two or three hikers, especially at lower levels.

The Rangers talked to all the hikers coming down from the mountains to ask where they stayed. Few were from the Dollar Lake or Rae Lakes area. One couple said they heard a big argument from people who seemed below Dollar Lake. Of Course, echoes in the mountains and valleys can shift directions. It's hard to tell.

The searchers went by the beautiful Mist Falls and through Paradise Valley. The scenery near Castle Domes was spectacular. The three major peaks of the Domes were a rugged and magnificent picture-taking area. The searchers only had a little time for pictures, but David and Josh took some time because of the scenery. They joined the John Muir Trail, and the Rangers pointed out that it would be seven miles to Dollar Lake. Everyone then took a lot more time to search everywhere along the trail.

David and Josh were elated when the search party leader said they would camp there because it was late. Before the sunset in the west, the Castle Domes were still in plain view.

"I can't imagine what would go through a person's mind that would murder in a place like this, Josh said as they began to unpack, "Looking at this beautiful place, I wonder if God was just showing off when He built Kings Canyon Park."

David shook out his tent, "I can't agree more. I've never seen anything like this before." David began to laugh, "I'm so tired, I don't even know if I can see the view or not."

Rod was busy at his desk when he received a cell phone call and recognized that it was from Cindy, "Well, look who's calling this morning, hello good looking."

"Hello to you, handsome guy. What are you doing for lunch today? I've got something to run by you today."

"I'm working hard at my desk, just waiting for a gorgeous woman to call me."

Cindy laughs, "Hey, that gorgeous woman better be me."

"Of course, Cindy, who else would it be?"

"Maybe that new admin girl you hired."

Rod chuckled, "I think Conrad has his eye on Susan."

"Oh really?" Cindy said, "Something new going on there? Anyway, I'll be there about 11:30. See you then, handsome."

Rod put his cell phone in his pocket. He had a big smile on his face. Susan Brentworth stood at Rod's office door with her hands on her hips.

"Rod, what have you been saying about me and to whom?"

Rod stammered briefly, "How long have you been there?"

"Enough to hear my name."

"Okay, you caught me; I was talking to Cindy and spreading some gossip," Rod said as he sheepishly turned away from Susan, "She'll be by around 11:30, so be good to her."

"You know, I'm good to everyone, especially Cindy," Susan said as she turned and returned to work, humming.

Al Fletcher was positively identified by the Fresno

County Medical Examiner. The word of Al's murder went through the Fresno community like wildfire. Al was known by so many, not only because of the fitness club but his work with the drug addicts in the area.

Everyone was talking about Becky Savage. What happened to her? Many people knew that she was with Al. The local radio and television stations were all talking about Al and Becky. The news was all serious.

The Park Rangers heard about it first and passed it along to the whole group.

Josh and David were sitting on a boulder by the lake, "I've seen these types of murders before. I bet there's a lot more to it than this one murder. It's too remote here to be random," Josh remarked.

David responded, "I also have a gut feeling about this one. We better keep on our toes."

The mood changed in the group from that moment on.

At eleven-fifteen, Cindy knocked on Rod's office door.

"Come on in, Cindy," Rod said as he stood and came around his desk.

"How did you know it was me?"

"A little bird told me," Rod laughed, "Through the office intercom. You look wonderful. How about a hug? I need one."

They give each other a way too long hug, but who cares...

Rod loosened his tie, which he never wears except on special occasions.

Cindy stepped back, "Why don't we take Susan along. I would like to get to know more about her."

"I thought you needed to talk about something?"

"What I have to talk about is not a secret. Anyway, it's a dilemma that maybe three brains can handle better than two. I'll go ask Susan," Cindy said as she was already out the door.

During the meal, Cindy asked, "Clint is having trouble getting into Med School. Is this a good time to talk about it?"

"Sure, let's have it," Susan responded.

"Okay, Clint has been trying to apply to different Med Schools for some time, and once they read about his prison time, they say *no thanks*. It doesn't seem fair."

Rod spoke, "You have to look at it from their perspective. I know how you feel, Cindy, but let's discuss what we can do. Can't your dad throw his influence into the game? After all, he's the Assistant Secretary of State, isn't he?"

Cindy looked at Rod critically, "Come on, Rod, this is serious. Dad knows all about it, but Clint wants to do it on his own merits. Besides, Dad doesn't want to jeopardize his position with the State Department by putting undue influence to get his son into a university."

"Maybe Rod was kidding, but you're right, Cindy. How about we finish our meal and head back to the office and think about this some more," Susan said as she put her napkin down.

Back at the office, they sat in Rod's office, deep in thought. Rod leaned back, scratching his head, "Maybe we can get a lot of people to sign petitions to send to these schools on his behalf."

Susan pointed her finger in the air, "Wait a minute, I have a dear friend who is the Head of Admissions at UC Davis School of Medicine. Let me write a formal letter using our letterhead, and you and I, Rod, can sign it.

I'll call him to let him know an important letter will be coming from the Carson Detective Agency."

Cindy had to use a tissue, "Thank you so much, Susan. Now I know why I like you so much. Are you sure it would not be too imposing on your friendship?"

"Not at all. We grew up together on the same street and went to high school and college together. I even went on a date with him a long time ago. Can't men and women have friends of the opposite sex? He would not and has not on occasions asked me for favors."

Rod sat there for a moment, maybe it was Parkinson's, but he finally said, "Susan, you *are* a jewel. I'm so delighted that you're part of our team."

Susan stood, and as she turned to go, "Well, is this a good time to ask for a raise?" She was out the door before Rod could respond.

"Susan doesn't know it, but that is the school Clint had his heart on attending."

Rod hugged Cindy, "You have been so good to me and for me. When I start having tremors, I think about you, and that helps and calms me down."

"Thanks so much, Rod. How have you been feeling lately?"

"Up and down, both physically and mentally. I think I've read too much about Parkinson's. It's depressing."

"You realize I'm here for you, don't you? You can call me anytime, day or night, I mean anytime, is that okay?"

"Okay," Rod said as he gave her another hug.

At the office door, she turned to go, and Cindy said, "Rod, you keep your eyes off Susan, your mine."

CHAPTER FIVE

Joe Brooks called Rod, "I need to come over and talk to you. When would be a good time?"

Rod responded, "I'm not busy now, Joe. You can come right over."

Joe entered the door twenty minutes later, and Jordan accompanied him to Rod's office.

Rod heard them coming, and he went around the desk, ready to shake hands with Joe as he entered Rod's office, "Let's sit over here," Rod showed Joe to a couple of plush armchairs facing each other with a coffee table between them, "Would you like some coffee or anything else to drink?" As they both sat down.

"Some coffee, please. I think I need some caffeine to help me."

Jordan was still at the door, "I'll get that for you, Mr. Brooks. Would you want some coffee also, Rod?"

"Yes, please, and thanks, Jordan," Rod said as he turned his attention back to Joe, "To be candid, Joe, you look like you've been hit by a truck."

Rod, my wife, Dawn, is falling apart, and it's worse every day we don't hear any news about Roger. I thought I would get away for a while. One, to be honest, leave home for even a few minutes. And the other reason is to get as much information as possible about our son."

"Listen, Joe, don't feel bad about wanting to get away. I can understand why. I don't know how I might deal with what you and your family are coping with now."

"It's not easy, Rod; I don't know how much more I can take."

"Joe, my dad told me something long ago when I was facing something hard. He said, 'God never leaves us, and He never abandons us,' Dad also told me, 'Nothing comes easy in this life. There will be valleys along the way, but we need to keep our eyes on the mountains.'"

"Thanks, Rod, but it is hard to even see the next step, much less the hills."

Rod decided to tell Joe about the body found, "Joe, what I'm about to tell you is to be kept to yourself. The Park Rangers found a body in the mountains, but it is *not* Roger."

Rod continued, "I have not heard a word about your son. David and Josh are climbing one of those mountains now, and they're almost at the point where the Park Rangers found the body of a guy from Fresno. I will let you know when we hear news about Roger."

Joe finished his coffee and stood, "Thanks so much, Rod, for your words of comfort and inspiration. I know you and your detectives will do your very best to bring him home. By the way, what did that guy die from?"

Rod came around the coffee table, "I don't know what he died from. I couldn't tell you if I knew how yet. Let me walk you out to your car."

With a heavy heart, Joe walked out with Rod, "I appreciate what you are doing to help us. I want to start paying your firm, so work up a financial paper and email that over to us. I know your people are not millionaires, so don't hesitate to quote us honestly."

"Take care, Joe, and I'll call you soon. I was not kidding when I said you're not bothering the Agency or me, so call when you want to."

The following day, it was becoming routine for Conrad to pick Rod up and head to their favorite restaurant. This morning Rod decided to order something different than his usual breakfast items. Pancakes, sausage, coffee, and orange juice rounded off his craving.

Conrad gave him a funny look, "Is this the new Rod Carson? Or is this a side-effect of Parkinson's?"

Rod smiled, "Haven't thought about side-effects of Parkinson's yet. Maybe it is."

Conrad chuckled, "I guess I'm just an old stick-in-the-mud."

Rod put his fork down, "Stick in the mud? What's that?"

"You've never heard of that? It means I'm dull, unadventurous, and I don't like change."

Rod thought about that for a moment, "Yeah, I can see that in you. Someday the right woman will come along and change all that."

Later that morning, there was a voicemail from the youngest of Jeff Marrone's boys, Ryan. It was hard and really out of place. He said something about wanting a lot of money for the building Jeff owned, or Ryan would give us notice that we had to vacate the building.

Rod was not happy. He chose to call his attorney instead of venting to Ryan. Rod had a difficult enough time with Parkinson's without dealing with this predicament. Rod knew that his former partner, Jeff, wanted the detective agency to remain on the premises as long as we wanted. Rod also believed that what Jeff said was in their contract.

Rod called Conrad into Rod's office, "Conrad, I want you to hear this. After listening to the recording, Conrad asked, "Is he out of his mind? This is not what Jeff wanted at all. Do you want me to head over there and confront him?"

"No, I'm calling our attorney; he can handle it," Rod said.

Conrad was still standing in the middle of the office, "I think I'll get a cold drink and head for my office," he mumbled as he left Rod's office.

Rod knew better than to say anything to Conrad in this mood. He picked up his cell phone to give his attorney a call. After the phone call, he called Cindy, "Cindy, I need some TLC today. Can you come down? Do you have time?"

"Do I have time? Of course, I have time. I'm not doing anything, and I need a ride today. What do you want to do?"

Rod responded, "Don't know, just come on down."

"Okay, I'll be there briefly; bye."

After Rod completed his call with Cindy, he reflected on the morning's events. About an hour later, the receptionist, Jordan, called Rod and told him his attorney called from his car and was on his way and wanted to talk.

Ten minutes later, the attorney entered Rod's office, "Hi, Rod; got a minute?" William Steinwood said.

Rod stumbled a little as he stood, "Bill, thanks so much for stopping by. I need your help."

"That's what I'm here for. I've already checked the paperwork concerning you and Jeff's merger deal. I have some good news, but with good news, there always seems to be some bad news. What do you want first?"

"Let's get the bad news out of the way."

Bill took a drink of water Jordan had given him, "Jeff willed the ownership of the building to his boys, Jason first and controlling interest, with Ryan owning the rest. Now, it's my opinion Jason will be better to deal with. I have also contacted Jeff's attorney, who agrees with my assessment."

"That's really not too bad news. What do you think is our next move?"

"Let me first give you the better news," Bill said, "Jeff re-did his will after the merger. Under the current arrangement, Jeff stated that the Carson Detective Agency would remain where it is at the direction of the head of the Carson Detective Agency. That means you will stay right here if you so desire. Of course, yearly lease commitment can be raised to a ligament amount. Okay, that said, here's what I recommend. I will set up a meeting between you, Jason and Ryan, and the attorneys. Jason is more responsible than Ryan – don't tell anyone I said that."

"That sounds great to me. I just hope Jason and especially Ryan agree," Rod said as they sat back and relaxed.

Bill nodded in agreement, "I think it would be better here. Maybe in the second-floor conference room. That is closer to Jeff's old office, and the boys might be more relaxed there."

"Let me know when and I'll be there," Rod said as they rose, "I'll be glad when the dust settles."

Just then, Cindy knocked on Rod's open office door.

"Hi Cindy, come in. This is William Steinwood, our attorney," Rod came over to put his arm around her.

After the greetings, Rod said, "Cindy, I'm glad you're

here. You need to be in on this; do you have a couple more minutes, Bill?"

"Sure do, Rod,"

As they all sat down, Rod began, "Bill, I don't know if you've heard, but I've been diagnosed with Parkinson's. I must revise my will or any other legal stuff that applies to my firm."

"I'm so sorry to hear that news, Rod. I will work up some papers for you and the Carson Detective Agency. I won't rush this but the sooner, the better. Cindy, It's so good to finally meet you. I've heard a lot of good things about you."

"I'm pleased Rod told you about his diagnosis. That should relieve his mind of at least one more thing."

Bill said, "I'll call you soon, Rod; hang in there."

When Rod and Cindy were alone, she kissed and hugged him.

Rod kept hugging her, "I seem to feel better already. Let's sit down and talk for a few minutes, I'm a little tired, and then we can go to lunch, Okay?"

Rod closed his eyes briefly, "Cindy, this disease is getting to me."

Cindy smiled at Rod, "Let me give you some good news. Dad called his doctor friend, and they are looking for openings now. We should hear about an appointment in a day or so."

Rod looked up at Cindy, "That is great news. I've been searching the web for answers, praying, trying a low-protein diet, and attending the fitness club, but that's hard. I know I should exercise, but I keep tripping over everything. I take vitamin E and oil treatments, and I even tried dancing. Nothing seems to help."

Cindy approached the loveseat Rod was sitting in and

sat beside him, "I'm sorry. I think the first thing you mentioned is the best answer, *praying*. God knows the answer to what is going on with you. I'm sure the doctor Dad contacted will have solutions and answers for us. Rod, I like the part about you trying dancing. Maybe we can be dance partners and go on that TV Show."

Rod laughed at that thought, "Cindy, the way I'm bumping into everything, you would be black and blue and green by the time we get to the end of the dance."

They sat there quietly for what seemed a long time. Finally, Cindy squeezed his hand, "Come on, let's go to lunch. That might make you feel better. Where do you want to go eat?"

Rod thought and said, "Taco Bell."

"I'm sure that will make you feel much better."

They both had a great laugh and were still laughing as they stood up, and the laughing continued to her car.

Jordan just shook her head as they went by her and out the door.

CHAPTER SIX

Conrad and Rod spent time in the Monterey office with Sue to catch up with their office paperwork and messages. Sue filled them in on Aaron's search for a CFO and a Vice President to groom for potential CEO at Sterling Inc.

New cases were coming in at both offices, bringing some confidence that the firm was heading in the right direction.

Rod stepped into Conrad's office, "There's something I need to discuss with you."

Conrad interrupted him, "First, I received a call again last night from Susan. Sandi and Eva had another argument before Sandi stormed off and left for the day. It was about 2:30; as you can see, that was way before time to go home."

"Okay, thanks; you and I can deal with that this afternoon when we get up there. I have some ideas to calm the situation. Enough of that. I'd been thinking about some long-range plans we must make before I get worse. I mean my Parkinson's."

"Rod, you're not even close to that."

"I'm not feeling bad now, but I can't wait too long. Here's my plan, and with your approval, I have asked our attorney to write up some legal papers. Conrad, I would like you to be the Executive VP of Carson Detective Agency."

"I think you should think about that for a longer time. I'm not sure I am ready for that kind of responsibility. You know me better than anyone else. Are you sure?"

"I've never been surer. I will bring you in on all major decisions to make you feel better. I would like you to continue as you have been but do more decision-making on your own. Conrad, you have come a long way. You have stepped up to the plate a lot more lately. And besides that, you dress even better. Now, let's go to lunch."

After lunch, Conrad and Rod headed north to San Jose. They started to plan their methodology concerning Sandi and Eva. Something had to give.

As they approached San Jose, Rod said, "Let's stop by the Brooks home. We need to see if there are any more updates about Roger. Let's get Roger's girlfriend's name and any other names that Joe and Dawn might have for us."

"That's a good idea; at least we can try to help David and Josh at this end."

Rod called Joe to see if they could stop at their home, "No, we haven't heard anything yet. We want to ask some more questions. Don't know if you have the answers, but anything can help. See you in about 15 minutes."

Joe and his wife look like a mess. They didn't seem to have the strength to do everyday work.

Rod was concerned, "Joe and Dawn, you must take care of yourselves. Worry does not change the situation. I know it's hard, but you have to continue on with your life. I've never been in your shoes, but I know what is good for us. We are working hard from this end. David and Josh are now climbing to the area to look for Roger. They are also looking all the way up there. The Park Rangers stop everyone they see concerning the whereabouts of Roger. I don't think it will be long before we hear some news."

"Thanks, Rod, for your support and for reminding us that this situation is not in our hands. We will try not to worry so much."

After Rod and Conrad gathered the information they wanted, they headed for the office.

When they exited the car at the office, Conrad said, "I wonder if it will be cold or lukewarm inside the office?"

"It really doesn't matter. We have to do something."

They each went to their offices to check on messages. As soon as Rod sat down, Jada knocked on his open door, "Come in, Jada, what's up?"

"I suppose you heard about the fight around here."

"Yes, I heard about it."

"What you gonna do about it?" Jada said with her hands on her hips.

Rod took a moment to respond appropriately, "Come on in and sit down, Jada. Let's have a little talk."

After Jada was seated, Rod replied, "First of all, That's no way to talk to me. I'm going to be blunt here. It's none of your business how and when I handle any problem around the office."

Rod could tell that that didn't settle well with her. She sat there for a while without speaking. She regained her composure and said, "I think I had better apologize. I'm sorry, Rod, I shouldn't have spoken to you like that. Please forgive me."

"You're forgiven, and thank you for apologizing to me. I have asked Conrad to do more on another subject. I am promoting him to Executive VP at Carson Detective Agency.

On that other matter, he and I will take care of that situation today," Rod said as he sat back, "Now I have something I want you to do for me. David and Josh need some help. I would like you to go to Fresno and check on the backgrounds of those missing Fitness Club owners. Also, anything else you can find out about them. David and Jose are in the mountains, so I'm not sure you can contact them, so let me or Conrad know of any news we need to pass on to them."

"So, I'm not getting fired?" Jada said as she got up.

"Of course not, Jada. You're a valuable asset to this firm."

"Thank you, and I really am sorry. Let me know if I get out of line again."

"I will, Jada, have a good day."

After Jada left, Rod called Conrad, "Do you want me to be with you when you talk to Eva and Sandi?"

"Yes, I do. We cannot allow this type of problem at Carson's. Jordan told me it got into a shoving match, especially by Sandi. I don't know how she will respond, but we must expect anything."

"I want you to know, Conrad, I will support you on any decision. Call them into the Conference Room, and I'll join you there."

Five minutes later, Eva came in and sat down. She kept her head down. A moment later, Sandi came in and marched to a seat far from Eva. Conrad looked at Rod and then at the two women.

"Well, Eva, you start off and tell us what's going on?" Conrad said as he directed his question to Eva.

Eva slowly started, "We used to be friends, but now it's different with us. It started off mildly. I think I said something wrong or something in the wrong way, but it escalated to what happened yesterday."

Sandi couldn't contain herself, "Yea, her and her big mouth, she's always right, I'm always wrong, and I will not have it around me."

Conrad drank water to quench his dry throat, "Do you think we can work this out and act like adults. I don't expect everyone to be best friends, but we cannot condone fighting at Carson's."

"No, if she doesn't change or you don't send her somewhere else. I won't put up with her." Sandi said as she pounded her fist on the table.

Conrad put down his glass of water, "Well, now, we've got a problem."

"Yes, you do." Shouted Sandi.

"No, Sandi," Conrad said as calmly as possible, "You have and are the problem. Eva, would you excuse us for a while."

As Eva left, Sandi was even getting hotter, "So, I'm the problem. What are you going to do about it." She shouted.

Conrad just looked at her for a few moments. "Here's what I going to do. Sandi, I'm sorry; you are through here. No one gets physical with someone else around here. Please gather all your personal items, and I will receive your keys and escort you from the building. This is not a playground where you can play with other people's feelings or get physical and get away with it."

With that said, Conrad and Rod stood and watched as Sandi stormed out of the Conference Room. Conrad followed her to her work area and received her keys as she gathered her belongings. She threw her belongings in a bag and, without another word, turned and headed out the door

◆ ◆ ◆

When the sun rose that next morning over the Dollar Lake mountains, all the searchers were up and eating. The sunlight was sending rays across and through the trees and boulders. Shadows narrowed as the sun rose. The sun's rays hit the Painted Lady peak and Mt Rixford behind. The mountains in the distance reflected on the quiet lake. It's a scene that could take your breath away.

David, Josh, and their searching colleagues soon stowed their food and sleeping gear neatly away.

David yawned and stretched, "It is quiet this morning, too quiet. I hope we can get some answers today. Look how calm the lake is today. I'm not as calm."

Josh yawned because he saw and heard David yawn, "I'm surprised that no one has found any signs of a struggle or anything else that could lead us in a direction we need to go."

When all the searchers gathered around the lead Ranger and Sheriff Deputy, the head Ranger began to talk about search patterns.

David and Josh's team were tasked with the Baxter Lake Trail. These two groups got together and decided that one team would fan out on one side of the trail, and the other would take the other. Sometimes, cliffs, drop-offs, or other obstacles would be impossible. This part of their hike would be strenuous. The Baxter Lake Trail was much less traveled and maintained.

When the radio check was completed, they headed out.

Jada was soon on her way for a two-and-a-half to three-hour trip to Fresno. She didn't know how long she would stay, so Jada packed for two weeks. She had a heavy foot, so she was happy when she made it through a speed trap.

It was the second speed trap about 15 miles later that a sheriff's deputy stopped her doing 18 miles over the speed limit.

While Jada waited for the deputy to come to her car, she remembered her conversation with Rod and her mouth. It was good that she remembered because this deputy was in no mood to argue with anyone. Jada just smiled and did actually as the deputy directed.

When he saw her detective badge, his frown turned to a small smile. The deputy asked what she was doing in the area. After she explained why she was heading to Fresno, he said, "I've heard about what's going on at the national park. How about you take it a little slower and be careful while investigating. Oh, and thank you for being so pleasant today. I've had a rough day so far. People don't like law enforcement anymore."

"Yes, you're right about that. I hope you have a better day. Thank you for the courtesy of not giving me a ticket. I *will* take it easy."

Jada was in a better mood and started singing along with her CD. Soon, she was pulling into her desired hotel for her stay in Fresno. She wanted to get to the Fresno Police Department to get as much information as possible before heading out for some detective work.

Inside the police department, she was directed to the homicide detective in charge of Al Fletcher's murder case. Juan Garcia greeted Jada with a big smile that matched his immense size.

She felt right at ease, and soon she was given all the details that Juan knew at the time, "We really don't have much yet. We're waiting for the Medical Examiner to complete her examination of his body."

"Any word yet of his partner, Becky?"

"Nothing as of a little while ago. The search party is going over the area as we speak. That's a pretty desolate terrain up there. I think it's going to take a while."

"Do you have a list of friends and family I can take? I don't want to step on what has already been done, but that would help me get on with my investigation."

Juan stood and pulled a file out, "No problem, let me copy what I have here. Let me know any new leads you might get out there if you would. We can work together and make our jobs a lot easier."

After Jada received the copied files, "You've been so much help, Juan. I have heard that in some police departments, private detectives can't get the time of day."

Juan laughed, "Not here. I have heard about the Carson Detective Agency. Aren't they the ones who cracked that big embezzlement case in L.A.? Also, the U.S. State Department big wig, who's boy was kidnapped?"

Jada chuckled, "Yes, you got it right. Thanks for your support; working with you will be a pleasure. Have a good day."

As Jada approached his door, she turned around and dug a business card out, "Here's my contact information. Could I have yours?"

Jada was thinking, *I wonder if he's married?*

Juan pulled out his card and wrote on the back, "That's my personal cell phone number, so use that anytime."

Juan watched her leave. *I wonder if she's married?*

"Susan, could you come in here for a moment," Rod said as she passed his door. "You want a cup of coffee, Rod?"

"Sure, and would you have Conrad come in also? No,

you're not in trouble."

Conrad followed Susan into Rod's office, and they sat at Rod's smaller conference table.

Rod started, "Conrad and I have been talking about several things lately about our agency. First of all, I have promoted Conrad to the position of Executive Vice President of Carson's. You know, Susan, that I have Parkinson's, and I have more and more limitations that prohibit some of my activities here."

"Congratulations, Conrad," Susan said and punched him on his arm, "That's great news, not about your illness Rod, but Conrad's promotion."

They all laughed, "I know what you meant, Susan. I will turn it over to Conrad to explain why we brought you here."

Susan turned back to Conrad, and he said, "Susan, as you know, there have been some changes around here. That said, we would like you to be our new Office Manager. David has been the Office Manager here, but because of his workload as a detective, he will be too busy to be the Office Manager."

"David knows about this," Conrad continued, "but he doesn't know he will be our new Director of Operations. He will be over all the personnel at both offices. He deserves this promotion. Now, your position will include a significant pay raise. With more pay comes more responsibility. You will be in charge of all administrative positions at both offices. What do you think?"

Susan sat there momentarily, "I don't know what to say; I haven't been here that long, so this is a lovely surprise. What about Sue at Monterey?"

Rod spoke up, "I'm sure she will be engaged soon, and Conrad and I think it will be very soon when she asks to resign. That means we need to hire an admin person there and a detective for the Monterey office."

"You guys don't know how much this means to me. You don't know that Larry, my husband, and I have a son with some physical issues. This promotion will truly be a blessing. Thank you both so much. We have been having some financial problems, but now, most of those problems will go away."

"You're more than welcome. We have seen an amazing work ethic from you, and this is the reward for all that work. Let us know if these issues with your son change so we can help. Because of your added responsibilities, you might consider Victoria or Jordan to pick up some of the workload. Or we could hire another person for that job." Conrad said as they stood.

When Susan left, Conrad turned to Rod with a huge grin, "So this is what it's like being a boss. This is much better than the meeting yesterday with Sandi."

Rod went to his desk, "Yes, Conrad, this is what it's like. This is what it's like to be the boss. Sometimes."

CHAPTER SEVEN

Aaron was in his office early Thursday Morning. He knew this was going to be a good day. He had called Sue the morning before and asked her to come down for a few days. Aaron also had his chauffeur pick her up after work and bring her to the hotel in Camarillo, CA. He didn't tell her he wanted her to be in the interview for the CEO position. Aaron also had a surprise for Sue, and he planned for a beautiful evening at an exclusive restaurant.

His secretary came to his office and offered coffee, "No thanks, Ann. Come in and sit down. I have some news for you. First of all, as you know, Dennis Gilbert will be here at one this afternoon for an interview for the CEO position. I'm very excited because I think he might be the one we hire. The other news is Sue will also be here for the interview. I'm sure you know by now that I care for her and want her to be a part of any major decisions we make at Sterling."

Ann put her pen and tablet on his desk, "Yes, I would say, like the kids say, you have fallen hard for her."

"Yes, and I want to make it permanent. After work, I am taking Sue to a nice restaurant and will propose to her."

"Oh, that's wonderful. I'm so happy for you. It will be hard to keep my mouth shut while Sue is here. I had the feeling it wouldn't be long before you asked her. Congratulations!"

"Thank you, Ann. Would you bring me the file on Mr. Gilbert and the responses about him from Carson Detective Agency?"

"I sure will, Mr. Sterling. I'll be right back."

"Ann, you've worked here for a long time. Don't you think you can call me by my first name, at least when it's just us two?"

Ann turned and looked shocked, "I could never do that. My mother and dad said it would never be right to talk to your boss that way. I'll try, but it won't be easy, Mr. Sterling," she said with a smile.

Ann was soon back in Aaron's office with the files he wanted. Aaron got busy and poured over the files again. Dennis's resumé was impeccable. What surprised Aaron more was the detective agency's only negative comment was Dennis had a speeding ticket when he was much younger. Even his divorce was amicable, and their children were given the very best life could offer.

Aaron called Sue, "Good morning Sue, you're not still in bed, are you?" he said, laughing.

"Sure, I'm still in bed, and I think I'll stay here all day," she said, laughing with him, "What's on the agenda today?"

"I'm having the chauffeur pick you up this morning. Is eleven a good time?"

Sue responded, "I've been up for hours. I had a light breakfast and waited for someone special's call."

"Well, now, who was that special person?" Aaron replied.

"Oh, some good-looking young pool guy," Sue said sarcastically. After a moment, she laughed.

"Well, that leaves me out; I'm neither good-looking nor young." Aaron said, "See you soon, honey. I can't wait. We'll have a light lunch here at my office. I'll order some Chinese for us, okay?

"Sounds like fun. See you later."

"Dress up a little; we're going to a fancy restaurant tonight."

"I'll bring a dress to change into later this afternoon. Bye."

Two of Carson Detective Agency's detectives, Marcus Peterson and Javier Ortega, arrived at the trailhead of the Rea Lake Loop trail and were met by one of the Park Rangers.

Marcus was the younger between him and Javier. But Marcus knew that even at 44, Javier could beat him in just about anything. Marcus also knew that Javier did not like Mexican food. That's why Marcus wanted to stop at every Mexican restaurant he saw on the way to Fresno. They are best friends, and they kidded each other unmercifully.

When they arrived at the Rae Lakes Trail Loop, they called Josh and David.

After some discussion, it was decided that Marcus and Javier would remain in Fresno and investigate Al Fletcher and Becky Savage. That would help the overall investigation

Conrad picked up Rod at the usual time in the morning, but Conrad noticed that Rod didn't seem himself, "Are you okay to go to work?" Conrad said.

"Yes, I guess I'm a little under the weather."

Conrad watched closely as Rod got into Conrad's car, "Do you feel like some breakfast or just some coffee.?"

"Both; I'll be okay. I had a hard night; I couldn't sleep much."

Rod seemed okay, so they proceeded to get breakfast. Conrad noticed that Rod was more shaky than usual.

They got to work and went to their offices, Rod in his office and Conrad in his new, refurbished office. Conrad was like a new man. He could conquer the world with his new position and the staff's support.

Conrad was deep into his work when he heard a big bang. He ran out of his office to find Rod face down on the floor. Susan came next and knelt beside Rod. Rod slowly turned over, and there was blood coming down his face.

Conrad hollered at Jordan, "Call 9-1-1 and come back with some paper towels or something we can use to clean some of this off his face."

Jordan was off in a flash, and soon she returned with a towel. It's hard to run in high-heel shoes, but she made it okay.

Soon, they heard sirens, and Jordan went to let them in the door. When they arrived at Rod, he was sitting up and wondering what the fuss was about.

The EMTs took over, and Conrad stayed right by Rod.

"No, I'm not going to the hospital," Rod said defiantly.

Conrad said, "You're going if I have to carry you."

Rod looked up at Conrad with blood still running out his nose, "That would really look funny, wouldn't it?"

Conrad looked at the EMTs. "Well, at least he's not unconscious."

Rod looked around, "You all, get back to work."

All but Susan and Conrad stood their ground. Rod

looked again at Conrad, "Alright, I'll go to the hospital. I don't know what I tripped on."

Conrad took aside one of the emergency personnel, "He has been diagnosed with Parkinson's. I think he stumbled and fell."

"Don't worry, we'll take him in, and I'll let them know of his diagnosis. These types of falls can cause other problems. They will check him over completely. Don't worry, I think he's okay."

Conrad had heard that kind of response before but would not let that stop him from going to the hospital. First, he made a call to Cindy to let her know. Conrad knew that she might make it to the hospital before he did.

After Aaron and Sue had their Chinese lunch in a smaller Conference Room, they entered Aaron's office to wait for the interview.

As Sue sat down, "Why do you want me in on the CEO interview?"

Aaron looked up, "Because I want you to be a part of my major decisions at Sterling, Inc. You never know; you might come and work for me sometimes."

"You never know, Aaron; I might take over this place. I mean, I know so much about what you do." She said as she wrinkled up her nose and smiled at him.

Ann knocked on Aaron's door, "Dennis is here. I'll bring him in when you let me know."

"Give us five minutes, and you can come in with him."

"Okay, Mr. Sterling," Ann said as she went to the waiting room.

Aaron was looking out the door, "I've asked her recently to call me by my first name when no other employees are around. She said something about her mother and father wouldn't let her. Whatever that means."

Sue responded, "That means she was raised right. You deserve respect and honor because of your position."

Ann came to Aaron's open door five minutes later and knocked, "Mr. Sterling, this is Dennis Gilbert, Mr. Gilbert, this is Sue, and she will be with us."

Dennis Gilbert was a distinguished man with flecks of gray in his dark black hair. After all the formal greetings were done, Aaron directed the group to a conference table that was much larger than just the four people who would be sitting there.

Aaron started, "Dennis, I need to explain why these two ladies will be with us during the interview. First, Sue is my girlfriend, and Ann is my executive secretary. I don't know if you know what happened to my last CFO and CEO."

"Yes, I do know, and let me express my condolences about the CFO and your son. I can't imagine how you can carry on after such a loss."

Aaron cleared his throat, "Of course, everyone in the country must have heard about the crisis here at Sterling. I hope that doesn't change your mind about doing this interview."

Dennis looked straight at Aaron, "No, it doesn't. I've checked on my own, and honestly, working for Sterling would be an honor."

"Thank you, Dennis. Now tell us some about yourself. Would you like something to drink?"

After shaking his head, Dennis began by describing his family, the divorce, and that he and his wife have an excellent relationship but not as man and wife. He talked about his education and where he has worked since college. Aaron, Sue, and Ann sat quietly, impressed by his demeanor and grace.

When Dennis had finished, Aaron began to ask some technical business questions, what Dennis would see as goals, and what the future would look like if he became part of Sterling. That conversation went on for some time.

Aaron thanked Dennis for coming in, and then Aaron asked Sue or Ann if they had any questions.

Ann was first to speak up, "I watched Mr. Sterling go through hell a couple of years ago, and I never want to see that again. After what happened, we cannot hire anyone without vetting them closely. I hope you don't mind if I'm blunt with my feelings."

"Not at all, Ann," Dennis responded, "I expected it, and I hope you did some major checking on anyone who wants to work for this great company. I'm not just saying that for points; I mean it. I feel that a company that doesn't do that is in for a lot of trouble."

Aaron said, "I made that mistake years ago and will not repeat it. To be up-front with you, I had a detective agency look into your background and many others.

Sue said, "I would only echo what Ann said. I have seen Aaron in the basement of sorrow, not only his former CFO but especially his son. We hope that William, Aaron's son, can survive in prison and that he will be home soon."

Aaron was moved by what Ann and Sue said, "Thank you so much, ladies. I have nothing more to add. Dennis, I will contact you tomorrow about our decision."

"Thank you for the opportunity to render my resumé and to come in and meet you, Mr. Sterling, and these ladies. I'm looking forward to your call."

Aaron escorted Dennis to the outer door and returned to his office, "Well, ladies, what do you think?"

Sue was the first to speak, "I like him a lot. He has the right mix to fit into your company."

Ann said, "I totally agree with Sue. I personally think he will be good for you, Aaron. And besides that, he is handsome. Wow, did I really say that?"

Aaron laughed, "I agree with you both, but I will wait until tomorrow to let him know. I would like some time to think this through. Ann, will you document this interview and our responses, except the one about him being good-looking. I'll have to keep an eye on you, Ann. I didn't realize what the time was now. Sue, you said you needed to change before our date. I will work here until you get ready."

At the hospital, Rod had lots of tests completed, and the doctors decided to at least keep him overnight. Rod was unhappy about keeping him there but realized he had taken a nasty tumble.

Conrad said, "Hey, Rod, how are you doing?"

"Like a Mac truck hit me in the head. I'll be staying here for the night. They want to make sure I'm okay."

Conrad responded, "That's a good move on their part. You did take a heavy fall."

Rod's phone rang, and he thought it was Cindy, "Hi, beautiful."

"Hi, yourself, but this is not Cindy."

"Sorry, Susan, I'm still not thinking right."

"Is Conrad there?"

"Yes, he is."

"Put the speaker on because I want to speak to you

both, and I'm glad you're feeling better."

"Okay, I've got the speaker on with Conrad's help. Go ahead."

"You and the attorney were supposed to meet with the Marrone brothers this afternoon. Do you want me to cancel the meeting?"

Rod took a drink, "I totally forgot. No, I cannot make it but Conrad, why don't you attend the meeting. You know all the particulars. Susan, there's a file on my desk about the meeting. You can give it to Conrad when he gets back to the office. Have our attorney there early so he can meet with Conrad. Thanks, Susan. Is there anything else?"

"No, and I'll see you later, Conrad. Bye."

"Any questions, Conrad?" as Rod set his phone aside.

Conrad stood to leave, "No, if I do, I'll call. Don't worry; I can handle it. Jason Marrone is more reasonable, and I'm sure he can control his brother.

Aaron was looking over his files about the company's finances when he looked up to see Sue. What a beautiful scene. Sue was wearing a cream-colored dress that showed the curves of a gorgeous 36-year-old woman. Aaron took a moment to take in that picture of her that he did not want to forget. She also had a trendy cream sweater draped over her arm. Her shoes were a classy high heel burgundy color to complete the outfit.

"I guess I better freshen up and change into something more fitting. You look beautiful." Aaron then went to his washroom

Conrad's meeting started on time, "I want to welcome Jason and Ryan today. I'm sure this brings back some memories to you both. I can tell you that those who worked for your dad miss him very much. Okay, let's get started. I would like our attorney to start by giving us the legal status of Jeff's wishes and this building's ownership."

Bill Steinwood started, "Jeff did lay out his wishes in a document I have here. I'm curious if he talked to you boys about what he wanted. Jeff said the Carson Detective Agency would remain on the premises until the building was sold. He also wished that any new owner would honor his request if the Carson Detective Agency wanted to stay. Jeff expressed that the Carson Detective Agency would have the first choice in purchasing this building. Any questions so far?"

No one spoke up, but it was apparent that Ryan was disturbed by what he heard. Jason seemed to agree with the document.

The attorney said, "I must add, and I have it documented that if the building is sold, it will be sold only at a fair local assessment of value. Are there any questions about this document?

Ryan could not take it any longer, "You heard what amount I quoted to Rod Carson, and I expect that we receive that amount."

Jason was quiet for a few seconds, "Ryan, did you not hear what Dad put in that last document? You are being unreasonable about this. We have enough money alone and don't want an exorbitant amount to satisfy our wants. Don't you remember what Dad always told us, 'It's not good to want what we cannot have or deserve? I think what Mr. Steinwood has read to us is proper and fair."

"Well, I don't," Ryan said as he pounded his fist on the table.

"Ryan, you're not going to like it, but you're out of line. Remember that Dad gave me the major percentage of our inheritance. I love brother, but this is not something we should fight over."

Ryan was upset and slid his chair back. Everyone thought he was going to leave. However, he cooled down after a moment, "I really thought this building would be our key to an early retirement."

Jason looked over to his brother, and after a moment, he laughed, "That's the craziest thing I ever heard – our retirement?"

Soon Ryan was laughing also, then the whole group.

The attorney spoke to Ryan, "Ryan, I won't charge you very much for this meeting, okay?"

Jason told Conrad, "I wish Rod was here, but I hope he is better. We did not know about his Parkinson's. Conrad, I would like to propose a resolution to what will happen to this building. According to Dad's wishes, we can keep the arraignment like it is now. And I believe Dad would want the building sold to the Carson Detective Agency. At a fair price."

Conrad was ecstatic, "Jason, Ryan, thank you very much for what I would consider a very successful meeting. I will stop by the hospital after this meeting ends to discuss it with him. There is a lot of planning we must do to come to some sort of decision. We will get back to you ASAP."

Bill Steinwood stood, "I think this meeting is over, and thank you both, Jason and Ryan, for your spirit, and I know your dad would be very pleased with his boys."

They all stood and said their farewells and left.

Aaron took Sue to one of the most exclusive restaurants in Los Angeles. He had talked to the owner earlier and secured a quiet table with a great city scene. Aaron was so nervous. He recalled when he took his first wife out to propose to her. Not quite the same because he needed more money then.

Sue and Aaron enjoyed their time eating and having great conversations. After the meal and dessert, they appreciated and delighted in a nice goblet of wine.

Sue remarked, "Aaron, this has been a delightful dinner. Can we afford to do this more often?"

"I'm happy you put it that way. I've been thinking lately that we need to do just that," Aaron said as he reached into his coat pocket, "Sue, will you marry me. I want us to be able to do this a lot more often."

"Yes, Yes, Yes, and Yes," she said much louder than she expected, "I'm sorry, Aaron, I love you so much."

The restaurant broke out in applause. Now, Sue was embarrassed. They spent the next hour drinking more wine. At that moment, nothing was more critical than for Aaron and Sue to be talking about the future.

As they got ready to leave, Sue looked lovingly at Aaron, "Now, what do you have to top that?"

CHAPTER EIGHT

High in the western mountain range, the Baxter Lake trail provides some of the most challenging mountain climbing hikes. The rugged path gains over six thousand feet before it reaches Baxter Pass. The switchbacks are rocky and steep and less traveled than the more popular Rae Lakes Loop.

Once a person reaches the top of the pass, the scenes are spectacular. Providing views of granite peaks and several sparkling, pristine alpine lakes.

This is the home of the Sierra Bighorn Sheep. These sheep thrive in the cold, rugged, and isolated area of Baxter Mountain.

Elizabeth woke up to the eastern sun that broke through the trees and cliffs near their camp high above the lake. Her thoughts were not on the scenery around them but what would be Derik's mood this morning.

Derik was nowhere around, so Beth dressed and started breakfast. The smell of coffee and food could be carried long distances through these canyons and cliffs.

It wasn't long before Derik showed up, and Beth could tell he was in a bad mental attitude. "What are you doing? Didn't I tell you to wait until I was here before you started a fire? You have no brains?"

"I wanted to have some food for you when you

returned."

"You never listen. What if people are coming, and I don't want them to know where we are."

Beth turned away from Derik and wiped a tear from her cheek, "I'm sorry."

Derik sat and ate his breakfast in isolated silence.

They had a great view of Baxter Lake and sections of the trail coming down off Baxter Pass. Derik carefully selected this location because he wanted to know who was around.

Elizabeth was quiet and planning. How could she escape Derik? It would take work.

Derik laid back with his hands behind his head. He was doing some planning of his own.

Sue was up and was getting dressed in her hotel room when her cell phone rang, "Good morning, husband-to-be."

"Good morning to you. I'm at the office and will call our new CEO shortly. What have you planned for today?"

Sue slipped on her shoes, "Ann said we needed to do some shopping today."

"I may have to call in another secretary today," Aaron said as he laughed, "I'll have my driver pick you up later. I'm sure Ann will be with him."

"Sounds great. Are you sure it's okay with you?"

Aaron responded, "Ann is excited about your adventure today. See you later."

A few minutes later, Ann came to Aaron's office door, "Remember, we have an interview with Janet Millard this afternoon at three. I'll be back by two. You still want me to be in on that interview?" Ann replied.

"Yes, Ann, I believe it's the proper thing to do, and I want your input on her. See you at two."

Conrad picked up Rod at the hospital and decided to go to their office.

When they arrived, Rod said, "Come into my office. I have something to talk about with you. It's about our Monterey Office."

"Want something to drink, Rod? Conrad said at Rod's office door.

"Sure, how about some coffee. Did I see some donuts when we came into the office?" Rod said as he licked his lips.

Conrad gave him the thumbs-up signal, "I'll be right back."

Soon Conrad entered Rod's office and, with Susan's help, had some coffee and a plate of assorted donuts.

It was quiet for a while because they were munching on the donuts and sipping coffee.

Rod put his coffee on the side table beside his armchair, "Conrad, I've been thinking about the Monterey Office and whether we should close that. I have mixed emotions about doing that."

Conrad also put down his coffee and finished his donut, "I know what you mean; closing that office has some good points, but you'll have to admit that the location is perfect for the southern region of California. And we have generated many more clients from the L.A. area and San Diego complex."

"You're right about that. My only thought is that we will be losing Sue soon. This office here also has generated a lot more business in the last few years," Rod sat back and took another drink of his coffee, "Having both offices makes business and financial sense. I'm also thinking about my health. Do we need to hire more people than the two or three at Monterey?"

Conrad looked closely at Rod, "Okay, you told me to come out and talk straight with you. If your health declines to where you can't work anymore, don't you think the people we have now will step up to the plate, and Carson's will go on?"

Rod finished drinking his coffee and was deep in thought, "I know you're right, Conrad. We have a ship that is sailing along in calm weather. But if this ship gets into stormy weather, will it make it to port."

"That's the funniest analogy I have ever heard. Where did that come from?" Conrad said as his head tilted back and had a hard belly laugh.

Rod laughed, "My dad said that a long time ago. You know how he loved sailing."

They both grabbed for the one donut left, "Okay," Rod said, "I'll split it with you. Seriously, you know what I mean. I know that if or when something happens to me and I can't work, Carson's will not fall apart. One person does not make a company. I am not indispensable."

Conrad was deep in thought, "I know you well enough to know you believe that. That's the quality in you that I like and why we have got along for these many years. I believe we keep the Monterey office and begin looking immediately for one quality administrative person and an outstanding detective. Maybe someone here would like to move there."

Rod agreed by nodding his head, "I agree with you. I knew I had made the right decision about you. Vice President today and maybe CEO tomorrow."

"Oh, let's not get crazy here. One day at a time, please. If you don't mind," Conrad said, "I'll start putting out some feelers for an admin person and maybe two detectives."

"Sounds good to me. Now get back to work," Rod laughed when he finished.

"Okay, boss, I'm out the door."

Rod went back to his desk and reflected on their conversation. He was highly pleased with what Conrad said about him. Conrad *could* run this company. Rod smiled and even laughed about the sailing dialogue. Where DID that come from?

Elizabeth had a plan. How could she pull it off without getting hurt? Time will tell, and it won't be long now.

She was getting more and more afraid of Derik. He was taking added drugs and could snap anytime, and she knew he could kill her. By now, she knew the trail down to Baxter Lake and the path that led up to Baxter Pass. But how would she get up to the Pass without Derik seeing her? Beth guessed that there was a back way to the pass. She remembered several lakes coming down the trail to Baxter Lake. Maybe she could find those lakes and make her way without being seen. Beth decided to do some hunting on her own to try and find a path to the top of the pass

Aaron called Dennis Gilbert, "Dennis, welcome to Sterling, Inc. I can't wait to get started on our working association. Let me know when a beginning date would be good for you."

"Thank you for the honor. The salary package looks great. I would like to review a couple of minor items with you. If it's okay with you, I can bring my personal items to my office on Monday. By the way, I didn't thank you for the company tour after the interview yesterday. I'm looking forward to our relationship and getting busy. By the way, how's it going on finding a CFO."

"Thanks, Dennis. We are glad to have you be a part of our team. We have a lady named Janet Millard coming this afternoon. She has impeccable credentials. I think she may be a great fit for Sterling's. See you Monday."

Aaron sat back and relaxed for the first time since before the embezzlement. He took a deep breath and exhaled. *Thank you, God, for your grace and mercy to me.* Now Aaron had to get ready for the CFO interview.

Sue and Ann were having the time of their lives. Who wouldn't when you shop in Beverly Hills. Rodeo Drive – is undeniably one of the most legendary streets in the world. Louis Vuitton, Hermès, and Chanel can all be found in this quintessential fashion district. These ladies were in vogue heaven.

Females forget that men can take just as much time to shop. Not where women like to shop. Men enjoy places like auto parts stores, sporting goods centers, gun stores, etc.

Ann almost forgot she must return to work by two. They may even have to stop by a bridal shop for a minute. Well, fifteen or twenty minutes.

Sue said, "I think we better return to your office. Aaron will fire both of us." They both were laughing as they exited the shop.

"It's good that we have a chauffeur to take us back. This was too much fun," Ann said as they found the limo to take them back

Aaron was in the middle of checking the files about Janet Millard and the feedback from Carson Detective Agency when Ann and Sue came bouncing into his office.

"Sorry, the traffic was so bad," Ann said deviously.

"Yeah, sure it was," Aaron said sternly, then slowly smiled, "Had a good time, I see. Spend a lot of money?"

Sue laughed, "We sure did and enjoyed every minute."

Ann said, "I'll return to work and prepare for Miss Millard."

"Stick around, Sue, and we'll go out for dinner again after the interview. Maybe around five, is that okay?"

"Sounds great to me. That will give me some time to look at what I bought," Sue said with an enormous smile.

Aaron was putting the files away when Susan came to his door, "Janet Millard is in the waiting room."

"Okay, you can bring her in."

A moment later, a very distinguished lady entered Aaron's office. Aaron was already on his feet, coming around his desk to greet her. She had exclusive business clothes with shoes to match. Her outfit accentuated her long black hair.

Aaron suggested they would be more comfortable at the conference table, "How about you start by telling us a little about yourself."

Janet was comfortable talking about her early years living in Texas and her family's dynamics. She told them that she attended the University of Texas and received her Doctor of Business Administration at the Naveen

Jindal School of Management.

Janet said, "I have never been married, and if I have a flaw, I'm married to my work. Although I have had some dear close friends and a pastor, caution me that I should ensure I have other interests that will balance my devotion to working."

Aaron responded, "I believe people in high-stress jobs should take that advice."

Janet continued, "At home, I have two poodles that are the joy of my life. I have a full-time live-in housekeeper, so I don't have to worry about them at work or away. I have maintained through the years that I attend a good church, and since I moved here, I have continued to practice my faith. I work out at a local fitness club and am an ardent baseball fan."

Aaron asked Janet about her work experience and what she sees as her goals at Sterling, Inc.

Janet talked at some length about not only what her job was at each company but also the good and not-so-good qualities of each company.

When she finished, Aaron said, "Sounds like you've had a wonderful life so far. I want time to think about this decision because I want to correctly bring someone into our company. You said you knew or read about our past CFO. You can understand why I'm a little nervous."

Janet replied, "I fully understand and agree with you. I'm sure you have other people you're looking at for this position. I want you to know I'm looking forward to possibly working here."

Aaron asked Janet some technical, financial questions, which she answered to his satisfaction. Aaron asked Janet, "Would you like to see our Financial Department and talk to some financial personnel?"

"I would love that opportunity; thank you so much."

"I'll get back to you soon with my decision. Maybe tomorrow or the next day. Thank you so much for wanting to join our company, Sterling, Inc.."

Susan then escorted Janet out, and soon she returned to Aaron's office, "She's got great qualifications. I like her, and she will be a great asset to us. Let me close the door. I know you've got some thinking to do. Let me know our next move."

CHAPTER NINE

Sunday afternoon is usually a time of relaxation. Rod was in his San Jose condominium watching a baseball game. His lazy boy chair was back; some snacks and drinks were on the small table beside his chair. The game was tied, and he tried not to think about his Parkinson's. Sometimes he had to hold his glass with two hands, so it wouldn't spill. Life is good! Then his cell phone sounded and scared him half to death.

"Hello," Rod said with a shaky voice.

"Hello, is this Rod?"

"Hi, Joe, what's going on?

"Can I come and talk with you? I need to get away for a while," Joe said.

"Sure, want to come over to my place, I'm watching the baseball game, and you can join me."

Rod gave Joe his home address and told him he had not heard anything about Roger, Joe's son.

Fifteen minutes later, there was a knock on Rod's door, "Come in, Joe, it's open," Rod shouted.

Rod could tell at first glance that Joe was not doing well. Rod offered Joe some snacks and a drink. They then went into the living area to watch the game. One team had scored a run, then in the other half of the inning, the other team scored a run. Still tied.

When the commercials came on, Joe turned to Rod, "I don't know how much more I can take. It's beginning to hurt my practice. My partner at our law firm is doing more and more work. He doesn't complain, but it has to be hard on him. They all want to help, but I don't know what they can do."

Rod responded, "In some way, I know what you're going through. With my Parkinson's, I'm working less and less. At times I feel helpless. I would like you to do something for me. I think it will help you and your family now. This morning at church, our pastor gave a great message on the Book of Job in the Bible. You know Job lost everything, and sometimes I feel like that. Well, I won't preach it to you because I can't. I would like you to stream that message from this morning. I feel you will understand why you are experiencing what you are facing now."

The commercials were done, and they were back to watching the game. Rod glanced over to Joe. Joe was deep in thought. Rod did not want to interrupt him.

It was nearing the end of the game, and they were both into what was going on. Laughing and shouting, eating snacks, and drinking more soft drinks.

The last part of the ninth inning was when their team was up with two strikeouts, and of course, the final batter hit the winning run. Joe jumped up and gave Rod a high five with Rod still in his chair. What a good time.

Joe sat back down and started to cry. Rod did not know what to do.

"Sorry, Rod," Joe said, "This has been the best time for me. Thank you. You know, you're just like your dad. He always knew what to say or do at the proper time."

"Thanks, Joe; Dad was like that. Thanks for the

compliment."

"I feel much better. It doesn't take away the hurt in my heart about my son disappearing. I know someday we will have the answer."

"Yes, we will, Joe. Thanks for coming over and watching the game with me. It's always better with someone else. I'm not sure Cindy would have the same enjoyment of the game."

Aaron called Janet Millard to acknowledge her as Sterling's new CFO. Before she accepted, Aaron asked her if she had received the salary package by messenger. He told her she could call him back with her answer.

Janet replied, "I don't have to call. I am pleased to accept your offer and am ready to start tomorrow morning. I also wanted to ask one question about the salary package. What is the transportation item that was listed."

"Oh, I wanted to surprise you about that. Your new chauffeur and limousine will be there Monday morning to pick you up."

Aaron continued by giving her the chauffeur's cell phone number.

"I'm flabbergasted about that. Is it alright for a sophisticated CFO to use that term?"

Aaron laughed, "You might be surprised at the terms I might use. Janet, we are going to have a great time. I can't wait to get started. See you sometime tomorrow, Don't rush in."

"Thanks again, Mr. Sterling. I'll see you there."

Aaron took another drink and thought, *I must break her of that, Mr. Sterling, handle.*

A little after lunch, Derik told Elizabeth, "I'm taking a walk. I want you to stay here in camp. Do you understand?"

"Yes, I understand. When do you want me to start the evening meal?" She asked.

Derik snapped at her, "I won't be back by that time. I don't want you to start a fire or turn on any lights."

"Okay, I'll probably be in bed. Without any lights, there will be nothing to do except sleep."

With that said, Derik stormed off.

Elizabeth had prepared for this moment for days. She had plenty of time to make her escape. Beth only had to watch which way Derik went. He took the path down to Baxter Lake. It was time to make the camp look like she had been there all day. Beth arranged her bedroll to look like she was in it. Now to get away while she had plenty of daylight.

She took some personal items but only a little. She didn't want any unneeded weight to slow her down. The trail she had planned differed from the path down to the lake. She headed almost straight towards Baxter Pass, which bypassed Baxter Lake. This route was more isolated, and it would traverse near some smaller lakes. Eventually, she would connect with the Baxter Trail and head west to find some Park Rangers.

Derik spent his time fishing at the lake, laying back on a large boulder to do more planning.

About one and a half hours later, Derik heard some voices. Sounds travel a long way in the mountains. It was from the direction of Baxter Pass. Derik was in a secluded lake area, and he doubted anyone could see him. Whoever it was, they had a lot of switchbacks to reach the lake. He decided to hide somewhere east of the lake. Not far, but enough to at least see their activities.

The two teams of searchers decided to spend the night at Baxter Pass. They had enough hours of daylight to put up their tents and gear. They were ready for a good meal before bedding for the night.

After dinner for the seven guys and one female Ranger, Josh and David walked to a nearby cliff that overlooked Baxter Lake and the area.

David sat on a bolder, "I wish we weren't looking for someone missing or a suspect. When this is over, I might return to this area for a challenging hike, just to take time to see these scenes."

Josh paused, "Looking at that lake, I wish I had brought a fishing pole. They make small poles that slide in and out for those who want to fish on their hike."

David looked at Josh, "You're just a wealth of information, aren't you."

"Yes, I am." Josh replied, "I used to go to some mountain lakes near the Mogollon Rim, northeast of Phoenix. Some of the biggest trout I have ever caught was up there."

"Maybe we can go there sometime on vacation. Sounds like a wonderfully peaceful location to hike and fish."

"Hey Josh, can I borrow those binoculars you have? I thought I saw some movement on the other side of the lake."

"You can't see that far; maybe it's a bear."

"Well, with these glasses, I saw something move. Can't see it anymore. It looked more human than animal."

"Did you hear that?" One of the Rangers shouted,

"Everyone is quiet."

"There it is again. It sounds like a woman shouting; maybe it's Becky Savage?"

A couple of the guys started to run down the side of the Pass towards this girl walking towards them. It took some time because of the terrain. When they reached her, they talked for a minute and then began to help her to their campsite. Twenty minutes later, she would have had a hard time because the sun was ready to set behind the cliffs.

Elizabeth Fox sat by the fire and began to tell her story. She related her fear of Derik. That's when one of the Rangers told her about the homicide victim, "I think Derik did it. He saw this guy he knew, and it was obvious that Derik didn't like him. What happened to the woman who was with that guy?"

"We don't know so far. We have many Law Enforcement people looking for her and others missing. We didn't know about you and Derik," the Park Ranger said.

Derik headed for his campsite. It was very quiet, too quiet. He looked in Beth's tent and tried to wake her up. That's when Derik discovered Elizabeth had disappeared. Derik was outraged. He looked around the area for a while but soon realized he had better leave the campsite. After all, what did Elizabeth know about him or what he did. Derik convinced himself Beth wouldn't say anything about him.

Derik decided to hide out for some time until those people left the mountain. If those people caused any problems, Derik knew there was a way back out to a reservation on the eastern side of the mountains. He went down to the lake and then east a couple hundred yards to a rise with some trees where he could hide. Derik didn't know how rugged the trail between Baxter Lake and the reservation was.

Derik had a safe place now, so he would start hiking out of there in the morning. When he took out his maps of the area, he calculated that it would take him at least two days to hike out.

The two teams that Josh and David were in decided that one of the teams would take Elizabeth back to Dollar Lake to meet up with the other searchers. At that point, they might request a helicopter to take her to Fresno for further questioning. Josh and David's team would go to Baxter Lake to investigate the area.

They knew that Roger Brooks was still missing. Becky Savage was missing. Derik Thomson was now also missing. What was a single missing person search became a much more significant concern. Anything from a simple coincidence to a possible serial killer case.

David and Josh's team sat down to discuss all the possibilities. They decided to double-check what each person in their squad carried as weapons. They also teamed up, two by two, to watch each other's back.

David said to the guys, "I did see movement on the other side of Baxter Lake. I wonder if that could have been Derik. He might be gone by the time we get there."

Josh said, "You could be right. Why don't we, when we get to the lake, divide up and go around each side of the lake. That way, we can watch each other and catch him if he returns that way."

CHAPTER TEN

Monday morning came, and Rod could not get out of bed. He called Conrad, "Conrad, don't pick me up this morning. I'm not feeling well."

"Okay, but you're not telling me everything, are you? Out with it, what's going on?"

Rod tried to set up, "I can't seem to get out of bed this morning. Let me lay here for a while, and I'll try again. If I continue to have problems, I'll call you back. Okay?"

"I can come over now if you want my help?"

"No, give me some time."

"Okay, but if you need help, call me."

Rod laid there for another hour, then tried to get up. Everything started to go in circles. His legs didn't want to work, and they failed him when he got out of bed.

His head hit the nightstand and knocked him out. Rod fell flat on the floor with blood oozing out of his head wound.

Janet Millard was in the office before Aaron's limo arrived at Sterling, Inc. Aaron could tell something was different this morning because a new potted plant was on his side table.

He then walked to Janet's new office, "Good morning,

Janet."

"Good morning, Mr. Sterling; I thought I would get an early start."

"Okay, Miss Millard, happy to have you aboard."

"I would rather you call me Janet. Miss Millard makes it sound like I'm an old maid."

"I'm glad you said that because you will start calling me Aaron, Okay?"

"Okay, boss," She hesitated for only a moment, "Aaron."

They laughed as Aaron came in to sit down, "Welcome to Sterling. I'm thrilled this process is over. Take your time getting settled, but we have some holes in our financial areas. I'm not asking for this information tomorrow, so when you come across items needing fixing, go ahead and fix them."

Janet appeared pleased, "I appreciate that, but my experience has been that the more people involved in a decision, the better. Your decision to let me talk to those in the finance branch of Sterling allowed me to know the kind of talent we have here. Your former CFO did not allow his top finance group to see certain things. I have already told them that I will never work that way. If someone sees a possible problem, they better come into my open office to discuss what they understand as the problem and the solution."

Aaron thought, "I don't understand his philosophy in that process. I guess I know now. He wanted to keep his activities private. I need to change my approach to our executives. Not to control them but to be in touch with what they do. I think I'll head back to my office and write up some actions to improve our working conditions and allow us to speak up when we see a possible crisis."

Aaron stood and, without saying another word, went

back to his office. He told Ann that he would be busy for some time in his office and that he didn't want to be disturbed unless it was Sue.

Cindy received a call from Conrad. He explained that Rod was not doing well this morning, "You know, Cindy, how stubborn he can sometimes be. I think I'll go back to see how he's feeling and encourage him to see his doctor again."

Cindy told Conrad okay, but that she will be heading there and she could take him to the doctor.

"Sounds good. I'll let you go to Rod's place. Sometimes I don't know what to do for him. This Parkinson's may worsen, and we may have to help him decide what comes next."

After they got off the phone, Conrad called Rod.

No answer. Conrad called again.

No answer. Now Conrad was getting worried. Rod always answers his phone. Conrad ran to his car.

He was heavily involved at his desk with papers all around. He was also searching on his computer when a quiet knock sounded on Aaron's office door, "Come in," he said a little too loud.

Sue peeked her head around the slightly open door, "I'm sorry, I'll come back later," Sue said as she turned to leave.

"No, no, come on in. Let me write down the thoughts in my head so I won't forget them. Please sit down.

Sue came in as quietly as she could and sat down on

the settee. Aaron continued to write on his computer for some time.

He looked up at Sue and smiled, "Good morning, sunshine. I'm delighted to see you. I have some ideas I want to run by you. I need your opinion."

Aaron printed off some pages he had been working on. For the next twenty minutes, Aaron explained his new leadership style for the executive team to Sue. As he talked, Sue felt free to interrupt him if she had a thought about what she heard. Aaron moved to the nearby conference table to jot down notes of their conversation.

After finishing the paperwork, Aaron returned to sit beside Sue, "You have helped me a great deal this morning. I am truly thankful that you're my fiancé. I'm looking forward to spending many years with you," Aaron said, kissing her.

Ann knocked on Aaron's office door, "Are you available now?"

"Yes, and Sue and I are just finished. What can I do for you?"

"I know you're busy, so I thought Sue and I could go shopping again. That was so much fun last week."

"Okay, you two, what have you got planned for today," Aaron said as he escorted Sue to the door.

Sue said, "We know you're busy with 'boss' stuff, so I decided we needed to get away and shop and have lunch."

Ann echoed Sue's comment, "Yes, we need to shop. I've already arranged with Lois to take over while I'm gone. She can order some food to come in for you. Just let her know."

"You've thought of everything, haven't you," Aaron said with a smile, "Go ahead, have a great time."

They were already outside the door.

Fortunately, Conrad had a key to let himself into Rod's condominium, "Rod, you okay?"

He heard a moan from Rod's bedroom, and he hurried inside.

Rod was still sitting on the floor, holding his head where he hit the nightstand. Blood was still running through his fingers.

Rod said weakly, "Conrad, get me a towel from the bathroom. I think I'm bleeding."

Conrad grabbed some towels, went to Rod's side, and bent down, "What happened?"

"I guess I tried to get up, but my legs didn't hold me."

"Let me look at that cut," Conrad responded as he pulled away the towel. I think I better call 9-1-1. That looks very deep."

"Oh, you don't need to do that. I'm okay, Rod said, still shaky.

"Cindy would murder me if I didn't call."

Conrad called and explained to the dispatch Rod's condition. They said they were on the way.

Fortunately for Cindy, she stayed with a friend who lived close to Rod's home.

As she pulled onto the street where Rod lived, an ambulance came around her and stopped at Rod's address. She pulled into a parking spot a little crooked. She flung open the door and ran to follow the EMTs into the building.

It could be for someone else – but no – they went in Rod's door.

One of the EMTs wanted to know who she was and why she followed them into this room.

Cindy quickly explained and went around him into the bedroom. All she saw was a bloody towel. She started to run to him, but a police officer held her back and told her to let the medics do their job.

Rod did not like all the attention. He strongly disagreed about going to the hospital, but Cindy overruled him. Rod was going. He heard the determination in Cindy's voice and the look on her face to not disagree with her.

Conrad held Cindy because she looked very shaky, "I'm heading back to work but call me to let me and the staff know how he is feeling."

Cindy tried to smile, "Okay, Conrad, I'll call as soon as I can. We must talk about what we should do next with him."

They loaded him up and soon were on the way. Cindy was close behind.

The same morning, high in the mountains above Baxter Lake, Derik thought he had better move again. Those people down there were doing a lot of searching. Through his binoculars, he was sure he saw a badge on several of the searchers. It's time to move. He was convinced that the trail down the eastern side of the mountains was just as challenging as it was getting to Baxter Lake. Derik did not like heading east. He would have to double back somehow to get his car.

The path he took didn't look like a trail. Loose stones, gravel, and shale rocks made a person slip. It was a challenging, unpleasant path. There wasn't as much scenery as there was coming up from the Rae Lakes Loop Trail. What Derik had to watch out for were the various prickly desert plants. He had to be careful, especially of the stinging nettle plant. He found little shade except for the occasional twisted Junipers.

It was nice when the clouds would block out the sun. But they soon passed, and the bright sun was bearing down on him. The only beautiful views were of the jagged granite peaks and alpine lakes. Derik did not care about that. All he cared about was getting to the foothills and finding a ride back around to his car.

He did see signs along the way that looked like either a Bobcat or a smaller Mountain Lion. He didn't know for sure but kept a sharp lookout. He did not want to run into one of those animals.

It was getting late, so Derik decided to sleep for the night. He had enough food for his dinner and a light breakfast.

Fortunately for him, he did not see anyone else on the trail. He would get a good night's sleep.

Cindy finally could go into Rod's hospital room after many tests were done on him.

"Hi, Hon," Cindy said as brightly as she could, "How are you feeling after all those tests?"

"Oh, they prod you here and stick you there. All with very tight-lipped, business-like expressions. And the hospital food was some good and some not-so-good."

"Yep, I know what you mean. Let me look at your head. Wow! That's a nasty blow you took. Do you remember what you hit?"

Rod gave her a funny look, "Ah, No, I hit something, and I don't remember anything else until Conrad walked into my room. I must have been a bloody mess."

Cindy asked, "Do you remember me showing up when

the EMTs arrived?"

"No, sorry, I wasn't feeling so good then."

"I was talking to one of the doctors here who waited on you, and he said it was probably your Parkinson's that made you fall. You know, we are going to discuss what comes next. You may need something to help you get around. You may not like that, but you also don't want what happened to you today. Agreed?"

"I agree, but I don't have to like it," Rod replied.

Rod's room seemed cold, but she knew they kept hospital rooms chillier. Cindy went to the window to pull the shades up to allow more sunshine. She did not like the odor of hospitals. Cleaning fluids and other unmentionable smells permeate the halls of medicine.

Two doctors walked in and wanted to talk to Rod. They assumed that Cindy was his wife, but she didn't tell them anything different. The older doctor said he was convinced that it was Parkinson's that caused him to fall. Depending on how some tests came out, they wanted to keep him there for at least one more day. They also wanted him to stay to ensure he didn't have a concussion.

Rod was unhappy but understood their reasoning: "I guess Conrad will have to be the boss a little longer. I'm in no shape to run a business now. I am fortunate to have appointed him the Executive VP when I did. Now, he also has the authority to make the decisions."

"Rod, you worry too much. Conrad is the best person in the whole company to run the business. I think it's about time you relax and smell the roses. Maybe that's a bad pun, but you know what I mean."

"Yes, I do know what you mean. Now, get out of here and let me sleep. Those pills they gave me are working. Thank you for your love for me."

Cindy reached over and kissed him on the cheek, "Love you, and I'll go do some shopping," She said as she gave him a wink and turned and left the room.

Derik woke up the following day very sick. He was throwing up and very weak. He decided it must have been the dinner he had last night. It wasn't much, just some leftover cheese and salami. Maybe those barbs he ran into or the water left in his canteen.

Derik did not hear a sound during the night or in the morning. He decided to wait until his stomach ache would end. No hurry now.

CHAPTER ELEVEN

The person David saw on the other side of Baxter Lake was long gone. David and Josh's team searched the area around the lake and the elevations. They did find the camp Elizabeth was talking about and the footprints of Derik as he left, heading eastward.

The team decided to call the other groups and tell them what they found. The Rangers, with their team, wanted to follow Derik. Between them, they had enough supplies to take them to the foothills on the eastern side of the Sierra Mountains.

Josh and David had to be extra careful because they needed to get used to hiking and searching in the mountains. They especially had to be cautious off-trail because there were lots of loose shale and gravel with medium size stones. Because of a fire sometime in the past decade, there were lots of dead and hazardous trees. Talus fields covered large areas of the slopes and were very dangerous.

There was an abundance of different plant life. Some areas were covered with purple sage. If David and Josh were not searching for someone, they would sit and take in the scene around them.

Their team leader called for them to meet together at the lake. The Ranger had heard from the search party's main responsible person and gave them the okay to go ahead and follow Derik. Their team gathered their gear and started up Derik's eastern path.

Josh looked at David, "I sure hope this trail is easier than the Baxter Pass summit."

David responded, "You got that right. I'm still tired from that climb," Let's get us a suspect."

In Fresno, Juan Garcia, the detective in charge of Al Fletcher's murder investigation, finished his interrogation of Elizabeth Fox.

Juan said, "Beth, do you feel safe at home? You're still shaking a lot."

Beth breathed deeply, "Frankly, I don't feel safe. He is very dangerous, and he knows where I live and who my friends are. I've got a new job at a bar, but he knows about it also. I don't know what to do."

"I'll tell you what we'll do for you. I have an ex-cop that will be your bodyguard until Derik is behind bars. Don't worry about the cost. The Police Department will take care of that. You stay right there, and I'll get him down here. Do you need anything else to eat or drink?"

"I saw that vending machine where I can get food and drink," Beth said as she got up.

Juan held his hand, "I didn't see you carrying a purse. Do you have any money?"

"Oh shoot, I forgot. I left that in the mountains. I was in such a hurry to get away from Derik."

Juan said, "No problem, I happen to be loaded today. My wife just gave me my allowance," He said as he escorted her to the vending machine, "Get whatever you want.

A half-hour later, a large man came into Juan's office.

Beth stood as Juan introduced her to her bodyguard.
Elizabeth was no longer afraid.

Carson's newest detectives, Marcus and Javier, spent considerable time investigating Derik Thomson. Elizabeth's investigation didn't last long. She had a lousy home life and did some drugs, but nothing major turned up.

Derik had a long crime sheet. Nothing significant, but enough to know he was heading in the wrong direction. Some jail time for minor crimes and drugs. The issue they noticed was the string of bad people he ran around with.

One thing that stood out was that one of his friends said Derik hated Al Fletcher. According to Derik's friend, Derik did not like Al trying to persuade him to quit drugs and running around with risky people.

The red flags went up. The detectives tried to call David and Josh. They couldn't reach them.

Around noontime, Derik stirred, and although his stomach still hurt, he needed to continue down to the foothills. He had a long way to go yet. He took his tent down and ate a bite or two of his food.

He was lifting his backpack to put on when a voice scared him, "Don't move or turn around. Keep your hands where they are, and don't make sudden moves," Josh said with his 9mm trained on Derik. The other two Park Rangers saw that Josh and David knew what they were doing.

Josh and David approached him from different

directions. He did not have a chance to run.

Derik said, "Okay, you got me. Who are you?"

David then told Derik who they were and that they would escort him down the rest of the way. David tried to call the other search party but was unsuccessful. His cell phone had no bars. The Park Rangers reached the other Park Ranger team with Josh and David with the National Park radios. They told them that they had Derik Tomson in custody and were taking him down the eastern side of the mountains. They also asked them to have some deputies ready to take them with Derik around the mountains to get back to the western trailhead and Fresno. They would make it just fine.

They did a thorough search on Derik's person and then his backpack. They removed a pistol and a long knife. They also confiscated some drugs. Then they tied a rope around his waist to keep him close. Handcuffs would not work because their subject could not keep his balance.

Of course, Josh, the jokester, had to say, giddy up, at least once. David laughed. Derik didn't.

Juan Garcia was sitting back on his office chair when the Medical Examiner called and told Juan that she had defiantly called Al Fletcher's death a homicide. Death by strangulation. Whoever did it strangled first to death, then shot him. The Medical Examiner also said there were ligature marks on his neck. Significant effects looked like a small rope. She went on to say there were traces of sleeping pills in his stomach.

That last information could be essential, or Al Fletcher just wanted a good night's sleep. Who knows.

Juan called Jada to give her the news from the Medical

Examiner, "Remember, this information is confidential."

"My lips are sealed. I'll only let the other detectives know about this. Thanks for the update. Anything else new about this case?"

"No, not yet. Hopefully, we can get some answers soon from the mountains."

"You're right about that. Take care. Bye."

Aaron told his secretary, Ann, that he wanted an all-executive meeting at ten. He also told her he wanted an all-personnel appointment at two that afternoon.

Ann returned quickly, "Everything is set for both meetings. Is there anything else you want me to do?

"No, except we need refreshments."

"Already on that, Aaron. Fresh donuts, goodies, and drinks will be ready for both meetings."

"Thanks, Ann, You know what to do."

Aaron finished his notes for the meetings.

Sterling, Inc.'s executives gathered in the company's smaller conference room. The first order of business was to introduce the new CEO and CFO. Most of the executives have already introduced themselves to the new Senior Executives.

Aaron looked around the room, "The first order of business is I need to apologize for what happened almost two years ago with the former CFO. I realize now that I need to change into the kind of leadership that this company deserves. I trusted everyone to do their job correctly.

Remember what President Reagan said, 'Trust but Verify.' I will be verifying and trusting from this moment on. I want each of you to verify what is going on around you. You can challenge me and my work if you see a potential problem I may be causing. How this is accomplished is a closer work environment.

Let me illustrate this point by using what is happening in sports today. When a flag is thrown on the field at a football game, the refs gather to ensure the call is correct. I'm not giving you yellow flags today."

Everyone laughed. Aaron went on, "What I want is open doors at Sterling. This afternoon, I will tell all the employees that they have the same right to come into our offices to discuss possible problems. I want to thank our new CFO, Janet Millard, for putting this concept in my ear when I hired her. No, you can't blame her if I get tougher sometimes.

The meeting went on for some time. Questions were answered, and clarifications were made.

Aaron threw a yellow flag on the conference table at the end of the meeting.

At the eastern side of the Baxter Trail, it was late afternoon. David and Josh's team decided to stop for the night.

They stopped by a stream providing cold mountain water and plenty of clear, reasonably level ground to pitch their tents. The first thing they did was handcuff Derik.

"Hey, what are you doing? How can I sleep like this?"

"With all the walking we did, you should sleep like a baby," Josh reminded him, "Set up your tent. You should not have any problem with that."

Derik grumbled and moaned but got to work. One of the Rangers started fixing dinner as Josh set up their tents, and David watched Derik.

Derik complained, "Hey, take this rope off me."

"Whoa, there, horsey," Josh said, laughing.

What happened in the next few moments was a string of curse words from Derik. Some were words that David had not heard before.

"Well, now, did we wake him up, Josh?" David said as he plugged his ears, "Do we have to put a gag in his mouth?"

Derik then gave them a dirty look but kept his mouth shut. He still mumbled some words David and Josh could not hear.

The sun was beginning to hide behind the western granite peaks. The team surmised they would reach the foothills by mid-afternoon the next day. Derik was handcuffed when they put him in his tent. David took the first watch. Josh jumped into his sleeping bag to slumber for the night because one of the other Park Rangers said he would take the last watch.

The only problem was that David almost shot the marmot that ventured into camp. That made the others jump up as the creature wandered away.

Aaron walked into the large conference room where the employees gathered for the company meeting. Aaron told the executives they only had to come if they wanted to attend.

Everyone stood as he entered, and he had them sit down. Some were sure it would be bad news, primarily because of what happened to the former CFO.

Aaron started, "If you haven't had a donut or coffee

yet, please get it now. We'll take a few moments to get comfortable."

After things settled down, Aaron began, "Thanks for coming on short notice. I have received some conversations from a couple of supervisors that you think I'm in a bad mood and ready to chew everyone out," He chuckled, "No, I'm okay. No one will be chewed out today."

They all seemed to give a collected sigh of relief and relaxing.

"I want to introduce our new CEO, Dennis Gilbert, and our new CFO, Janet Millard. You will get to know them as time goes by. For the first time in two years, we now have a first-class executive team that will lead us into the future.

Aaron drank some water, "I told the executive team this morning that we will have a new leadership style. I needed to make a change in myself to develop an approach that would enhance the trust I have in everyone. I also told them what President Reagan said some time ago, 'Trust but Verify.' I trusted the former CFO to the point that I did not verify. I don't believe that will happen again. All of us need to check on each other. Not in a nosey way, but if something does not seem right to you, you have to check it out. It's okay to say, 'Does this seem right with you?' or 'This is what I see.'"

Aaron resumed, "I would like to give you the freedom to challenge when something seems wrong. Let me give you a sports analogy. In a football game, a ref will sometimes throw a yellow flag. The refs will get together to make sure the call is right. Why can't a business do the same thing? No, I'm not handing out yellow flags."

They all laughed. Aaron described his new philosophy

in a humorous and educational technique.

He asked for any questions, but there were none, "Okay, I think we're done today. Finish up the donuts and drinks, and I would like to have this kind of meeting every six months or so. Thank you, and have a good rest of the workday.

Juan Garcia called Jada again, "What are you doing for dinner? I would love to take you out to a nice restaurant."

Jada did not hesitate, "I would love to have dinner with you. Is the restaurant a dress-up type place?"

"It's a casual dress-up restaurant. Something like what you wore to my office the other day would be fine. How about six fifteen when I pick you up, Okay?"

"I'm looking forward to it, see you later. Bye."

Juan was smiling as he got off the phone. He told himself *I had yet to ask her if she was married.*

CHAPTER TWELVE

Rod was released from the hospital on the morning of the third day. They kept him an extra day because of his concussion.

It was not too soon for Rod. His patience was thin, and all the hospital staff knew it because he complained about everything.

Cindy picked him up, and his mood quickly changed. Rod was fuming as they got into Cindy's car, "Cindy, you can't believe what I had to go through in that hospital. I was tested here and there and poked way too many times. The food, I think, was brought over from the nearby prison. They woke me up all night to give me something or check this or that. Oh, and the lack of privacy. When will they make a gown that covers all your private areas."

Cindy did not say a word. She just kept driving.

"And besides that, they kept me another day for no reason. Just have a little headache. And besides all that, my TV didn't work. No one picked up my cell phone and brought it with them when I fell. Now, I tell you, what can a guy do without his phone."

Rod finally looked at Cindy, "You're very quiet; what's the problem?"

"You didn't let me get a word in anywhere. Have you finished complaining about the hospital?

Cindy gave him a little smile. Rod was still for a few moments. "Well, I had to get that out of my system."

"That's the most complaining I have ever heard from you. I hope you feel better," Cindy said sarcastically.

Rod only sat there without saying a word. Then he laughed, "I guess that sounded pretty bad, didn't it."

"Yes, it did."

"I think you would feel that way too."

"No, I wouldn't."

"You're right. You wouldn't feel that way."

"Rod, you had a terrible fall in your bedroom. I think you're very fortunate to have only a mild concussion. Hospitals and medical staff are there for you and your medical condition. I thought they had wonderful staff to help you when I was there."

Rod was again quiet for a minute, "I guess you're right. I was feeling sorry for myself. Can't a guy do that once in a while?"

"No."

Rod was quiet again.

Then he spoke, "Can we stop at Toco Bell for lunch?"

Sue was up and ready for Aaron to pick her up. It was a beautiful morning in Camarillo, CA. The fragrant odors from the fruit trees and strawberry fields nearby smelled so good it would make you hungry. That part of Southern California generated a lot of the nation's produce. The strawberries grown there are featured as some of the biggest and best around.

Sue saw Aaron's limousine pull into the space near the hotel's main door. She laughed when she saw Aaron get out of the driver's seat.

"What are you doing? Don't you have a driver?" Sue said, still laughing.

"It's been a long time since I have driven that boat, and I told my driver to take the day off," Aaron replied as he removed the driver cap that was too big for him. He ran around to open the back door, so Sue could get in. She continued to laugh.

"You're a kick, Aaron. On chauffeur, and take me to my castle."

Aaron curtsied and returned to the driver's seat, "Well, my lady, are you ready for a glorious day with your subject?"

"Yes, I am, my lord. First, take me to yonder liquid gold bistro."

Aaron thought for a minute, then laughed, "Oh, Starbucks. On our way, my lady."

In Fresno, Javier and Marcus had finished their investigation of Derik the day before and were having breakfast.

Javier finished his coffee, "I still feel that Derik has something to do with Al Fletcher's murder. He had terrible feelings toward Fletcher, which might have led Derik to finish him off in the mountains. I'm sure he thought no one would know what happened."

"You could be right. I don't know. Derik was bad, but I don't know if you can connect the dots from Derik to Fletcher's murder. I guess murders have happened with less motive," Marcus said.

Javier put his napkin down, "I wonder if the Fresno PD has come up with anything new," he sat back, "We haven't heard from David and Josh. One of the Park Rangers said that David and Josh would follow their lead on Derik."

"I think we ought to head up there in case they need some help," Marcus said as he put a credit card on the table, "It makes me nervous that we cannot get ahold of David and Josh."

They paid their bill and headed for the car. Javier tried again to reach the detectives in the mountains, "I'm sure we can't get them where they are. Let's stop by the hotel and get our gear. I would like to hike today. Maybe we'll run into them on the way.

It didn't take long to reach Roads End and the trailhead for the Rae Lakes Loop trail. They told the deputies at the trailhead who they were and where they were going. They asked if they had heard anything from the other two detectives.

The answer was negative. Marcus and Javier changed into more comfortable clothes and hiking shoes and were on their way

The tremors Rod was having were getting worse. Cindy decided to take him to her home so he could get some rest. She also called Conrad and told him what she was going to do. After getting some extra clothes at his place, Cindy headed for Napa. Rod's head was hurting, so he leaned the seat back to close his eyes and rest.

Rod's symptoms were going downhill. The tremors, muscle rigidity, slow movement, and impaired balance took a toll on him. A toll that affects the body and the mind. He had read enough about Parkinson's to know these disorders would worsen. Maybe googling about the disease is not a good thing.

They soon reached Cindy's home, and she helped him

inside. The Royston home was a beautiful massive home on several levels. They had a lovely bedroom suite on the first floor where she took Ron. Cindy closed the blinds, covered Rod with a blanket, and shut the door to let him rest.

Cindy found her mom and told her where she had put Rod and his condition. They were in an upstairs sitting room. Cindy collapsed on the couch near her mom. Cindy started crying. Her mom could be strict sometimes, but she knew seeing Ron this way was extremely hard. She covered Cindy with a throw blanket and let her cry and rest.

Aaron turned on the air conditioner and then lit the gas fireplace. It was cool enough so they could snuggle on a loveseat near the fireplace.

Sue took out her quilting bag and continued making a blanket, "I want a nice blanket for our bedroom."

Aaron gave her a loving look, "I want to ask you something. I can't wait too long before we are married."

She put down her hooks, "We haven't discussed this yet. What did you have in mind.?"

With a severe face, Aaron turned to Sue and said, "Two months from Saturday morning."

Sue was at a loss for words after what seemed a very long time, "Wow, that's short; I mean, there's so much to do. Who are we going to get to stand with us? Who will give me away? What am I going to wear? Aaron, what about the invitations? The church, where will we get married on such short notice? What about my work? I can't leave Rod on such short notice."

Sue took a deep breath. Aaron put his arms around her.

"We will work all that out. You know I've been spending more time with your children. They even asked me when I was going to marry you. I've spoken to my pastor here in town, and that date is open. He penciled it in. Ron and Conrad are so excited to see us get married."

"You already told them?"

"No, I didn't tell them a date, but they encouraged me to hurry up."

"I know those guys would say something like that," She laughed.

Sue put her quilting bag on the floor and turned on the loveseat to face Aaron. She was so excited; words did not come easy. But her smile betrayed what she was feeling inside. Pure panic!

They talked about the wedding for the next two hours, the who, what, and where, but not the why.

Then they each went separately in Aaron's huge home to make phone calls.

Sue went into the den to call her children, who were now seven and five. They were so excited. She talked to her mom until she said she had to make other calls. Next, she had to call Ann, Aaron's secretary. Next, Rod and Conrad, Cindy had Rod's cell phone because she wanted him to get some rest. Cindy got the surprise of her life when Sue asked her to be her Maid of Honor. They talked about who else could be in the lineup.

Aaron also called Ann and told her to put that date on the calendar. Ann was also informed that Dennis Gilbert, their new CEO, would be in charge for at least a month.

Aaron called his son, James, about the plans. He said he wished William was not in prison for this occasion. He also called his brother and some close friends about his decision to marry Sue.

After they both finished contacting family and friends, they met again in the living room.

They snuggled together again and spoke quietly for a long time about the future.

Finally, Aaron looked at the clock on the mantle, "Sue, it's almost midnight. Why don't you stay here tonight."

"No, Aaron, we better not. Let's make our wedding night something special. I know that's old fashion, but I'm an old fashion girl."

"You're right. I'll take you down the hill to your hotel. Let's go.

Rod woke up and didn't know where he was. He lay there until the fog went away. Rod got up very slowly. He didn't want anything to happen to him like at his place.

Rod managed to get his bearings and slowly leave where he had slept. He found Cindy and her mother, Shirley, fixing dinner. Fortunately for Cindy and Shirley, they were not talking about Rod then.

They jumped when he spoke, "Did I sleep all day?"

Cindy regained her composer, "Yes, sleepy head. I checked on you a couple of times. You were sure restless. How do you feel?"

"I think I'm okay," Rod responded, "Thank you for using your bedroom. I needed the rest."

Shirley turned and looked at Rod, "Why don't you go into the family room and turn on the TV. We'll let you know when it's time to eat."

Rod did as he was told. With the TV blaring, Rod could tune out what was flying around in his head. He stretched out on the sofa with his feet dangling off the edge. A soft couch pillow felt good. He would have fallen asleep if the

TV wasn't on.

A short time later, Cindy brought in a tray of food for Rod, "We thought comfort food would be the best for you this afternoon. Let me go get a tray, and I'll join you."

On the couch, Cindy said, "Can I ask for the blessing on our food?"

"Ah, sure, go ahead," Rod said apprehensively.

Rod watched Cindy as she bowed, "Lord, thank you for this food. May it bless our bodies. Thank you for bringing Rod safely here to our home. In Jesus name, Amen."

Rod didn't close his eyes until halfway through her prayer.

"Thank you, Cindy, for that prayer. Now, I know why I love you so much." Rod said as he took a bite of his food.

He didn't see the tear roll down Cindy's cheek. She wiped it away with her napkin. She was so joyful.

After dinner, Cindy took the trays back to the kitchen and came back to sit by Rod. They talked and talked until it was time to sleep.

Rod looked at her, "After sleeping all day, I don't think I can sleep yet. I think I'll go in the den a write some notes."

"Okay, Rod, I'll see you in the morning. Love you."

"love you, too. Night.

Marcus got word that David and Josh were taking their suspect, Derik, down the other side of the mountain range. They were halfway up to Dollar Lake when they saw the magnificent Castle Domes.

These domes rise above Castle Domes Meadow to ten thousand, eight hundred feet. These granite peaks were some of the most rugged in the area.

Marcus and Javier continued the climb to Dollar Lake,

another eight miles. They would have to rest often because of the switchbacks and steep climb.

Marcus took out his water at one of the rest stops and drank, "I'd like to see what it's like on the other side of those Domes. It looks tough getting where we want."

"No problem, let's take an extra day or two. We're strong, and I know we can make it," Javier responded.

Their climb from Castle Domes Meadow to Dollar Lake was another fifteen hundred feet higher. That part of the hike was more dangerous and burdensome. They made it in time to set up camp and eat before they crashed into their tents for the night.

CHAPTER THIRTEEN

Sue did not sleep very well. Tossing and turning with the thoughts of weddings rolling through her mind. She got up at five and took a long shower. Sue had to admit she was excited and panicking because of the short time before her wedding.

WEDDING! *What do I do now?* Ann would help her. Sue tried to get dressed but kept putting things in the wrong places.

"Okay, get yourself together, Sue," She said out loud. She looked around as if someone would hear her. Of course, no one else was in her hotel room. She sat on her bed until reality came back into her mind.

Sue's phone rang then and in her state of mind, was it really her phone or only in her mind. After the fifth ring, Sue realized it *was* her phone.

"Hello," She said with a shaky voice.

"Sue, you okay? You don't sound right."

"Oh, Aaron, No, I'm okay. Just had a hard night trying to get some sleep. I guess I'm so excited about our plans that my mind kept thinking about different issues."

"Sue, everything will be okay. Take a deep breath, and I'll be over.

Rod needed to go to his San Jose office. Cindy and Rod decided to go to the Sunshine Café in Napa Valley for breakfast before they headed to San Jose. While they were eating, Rod received a call from Conrad reminding Rod that the both of them had to go to Monterey for some interviews.

Cindy remarked, "I'll just do some more shopping after I drop you off at work."

Rod sarcastically said, "Is that all you ever do, is go shopping? You should have everything by now," He was kidding and then laughed.

"You want me to look pretty, don't you?"

"I was just kidding. Go shopping. Have fun."

The ride after breakfast to Rod's office was full of conversation about their future and about Rod's upcoming appointment with the Neurologist. Cindy was worried that Rod would have some depression like some people with Parkinson's have.

When they arrived, Rod reached over and kissed her before getting out of the car, "Thanks for taking care of me so well. I really appreciate it."

"You're welcome. See you soon."

Rod found Conrad in Conrad's office. Rod came in with his coffee and sat down, "What's going on? Any new cases?"

Conrad found a sheet of paper and handed it to Rod, "We had a few calls this morning. Another missing person case. Two more possible divorce cases. They both want our detectives to follow their mates because they are certain their spouses are unfaithful. Rod, doesn't anyone have a good marriage anymore?"

Rod thought momentarily, "Do you have anyone on either case yet?"

"No, we only have Jerry, Eva, and me in the office until the others return from Fresno. I told Eva about one of the cases, and she's already on it. She thought a Hispanic could follow without being noticed by another Hispanic. The reasoning sounded good, so I told her to go for it. I told Jerry about the other missing case, and he's fired up for that one."

"The other divorce case must wait until we return from Monterey. I'm heading for my office to clear out messages and emails. I'll be ready to go in half an hour," Rod said as he stood and headed out Conrad's office door.

Cindy was deep into her shopping when she received a call from her mother, "Yes, Mom, I did not forget about the dinner party tonight. No, I will be home in plenty of time to dress up and look as cute as my mother," Cindy laughed and pushed the call-ending button. Her mother is constantly worried that her family will be late for everything. Cindy laughed again because it was her mother who was always late. Cindy thought her mother would be late for her own funeral.

With her hand clutching several packages, Cindy headed for the door. She finally opened the door and ran right into a gorgeous blond man. Of course, she dropped some of her boxes, and their heads bumped when she bent down to pick them up.

He finished picking up her packages, "Can I help you carry a few of these to your car?"

"That would be nice. I promise I won't hit you again," Cindy responded embarrassingly.

As they reached Cindy's car, she opened the trunk and deposited her bags. She was still uncomfortable when he spoke, "Hi, my name is Cory, and I forgot why I was even going to that store. I'm sure I will remember in a moment."

"Hi back to you, and thank you for picking up my packages. My name is Cindy, and I forgot my last name."

They both laughed as he shook her hand, "I guess I had better go because I'm sure you must do more shopping. Do you need any help?"

Cindy gained her composure, "No, I'm okay now. Maybe we can bump into each other some other time. Oh, I shouldn't say that. Bye."

Cory opened the door for her. As she got in, he said, "I would love to *bump* into you again. Have a great day."

She sat there because she couldn't find her keys. When Cindy saw them, she waved at Cory and started to back up, almost hitting him.

Could this day go any worse? He sure was good-looking.

The trip to Monterey was uneventful except for Conrad and Rod's weird conversation.

Conrad started by saying, "I need to get married."

Rod looked at Conrad sheepishly, "What brought that on?"

"Oh, I see lots of folks getting married and soon divorced. I'm divorced, but I think I could be a good husband now. I've learned a lot. You have taught me so much."

Rod chuckled, "Conrad, I've never been married. How could you learn from me about marriage."

"I know you've never been married, but how you treat Cindy best. That kind of relationship was never in my marriage."

"That's a great compliment, Conrad. I'll start looking right away for a woman for you."

"Now you're funning me. I'm serious. It's about time I settle down with a wife."

Rod snickered, "Like I said, I'll start looking."

Conrad could not talk for a while. Rod looked at him, "Okay, I'll be serious. That's great, Conrad. Are you looking now for one?"

"This may surprise you, but I went to church Sunday. All I could see were couples. You know, man and wife. They all seemed happy."

"I'll let you in on a secret. Just because a person attends church doesn't mean everything is fine at home. Search your heart; God will lead you to the right person. Church is a good place to start, but be careful. You need to get below the surface to see what they are like."

Rod tried to show Conrad the pitfalls and the enjoyment of dating and, hopefully, marriage. Rod revealed some of his thoughts about his parents. They had a perfect life together. Conrad said that his own family was dysfunctional, especially his dad.

Conrad cherished that conversation.

Soon, Conrad's car pulled into the Monterey office parking lot. Sue met them at the entrance and advised them that one of the interview persons was already there. "I really like her," Sue said as she escorted them into the conference room.

"Hello, Monique, sorry we're late. Give us a moment to put our stuff in our offices, and we'll be right back."

"No problem," Monique said with the cutest smile.

Conrad and Rod soon entered the conference room.

Sue asked them, "Do you want something to drink?"

Conrad and Rod said at the same time, "Coffee, please."

They all laughed. Rod said, "I guess we want coffee. Let's get down to business, Monique. Tell us a little about yourself."

She put her glasses on the table, "I'm 43 years old, and I have a wonderful husband, Jerry. He is a professor at Monterey Peninsula College. We moved here from LA when he was hired at MPC. We have no children. I had some minor jobs in the LA area. Then I went to UCLA and received a bachelor's degree in administration."

Conrad replied, "What made you apply here at Carson's?"

"My husband read all about your agency a couple of years ago. So when I saw your sign outside, I told myself I wanted to work there. We don't need the extra money, but it would be nice to have some extra spending money. It sounds exciting,"

Rod laughed, "If you ask most police officers and detectives what work is like. You get an answer: 'There are lots of boredom with moments of panic,' Conrad, you want to tell her?"

Conrad cleared his throat and handed her a sheet of paper with the salary and benefits. "If you agree with that purposed salary and benefits, it is our pleasure to welcome you to Carson Detective Agency."

Without hesitation, Monique responded, "Yes, I agree. When do I start?"

Rod replied, "Let's see, it's Thursday; how about Monday. Sue will happily show you around the place and set you up with one of our desks. Sue is engaged now, so we don't know how much time she will give us. I think the wedding will be soon, but she has agreed to help you."

"Wonderful, see you Monday."

Conrad stood with her and escorted her to the door.

When he returned, "Rod, she will be good for us. Very intelligent and very stable."

Rod grabbed his coffee cup and stood. He was unsteady, so he just stayed there until he felt better, "I agree. One down and one or two to go. Did Sue tell you when our next interview was coming in?"

"Yes, one at ten and another one at eleven."

"Come and get me for the next interview, Conrad. I need to check my messages in my office."

"Okay, I will"

In Rod's office, he sat back in his chair and turned to his favorite picture window. *Another day in paradise*, he thought.

One message was from Joe Brooks, wanting to know if there was news about his missing son. Another voice message was from the Neurologist's office, reminding him of his upcoming appointment.

Twenty minutes after ten, Conrad entered Rod's office and closed the door. He had a very disconcerting smirk on his face.

Rod looked up, "What's going on with you? You look like you just received your final notice."

"The next interview for the detective is here. No, don't get up. This guy is as drunk as a skunk. Sue gave me a dirty look, shaking her head no. I got the point. What do you want me to do."

Rod said with a devilish grin, "Go interview him. What does his résumé look like?"

"I'm afraid to look at it."

"Well, look at it and take it in there with you. If it's as

bad as you think, show him the road or call the police."

Conrad did as Rod had told him. He called the police because this guy had driven there. His résumé was good, too good. Conrad noticed that this guy's workplaces were short-lived. No wonder!

The local police came and put him in handcuffs, and they were escorting him out of the office when their second interview person went in the door. He turned around.

Conrad yelled, "It's okay. You must be Larry. Come in."

Aaron was in his office in LA but was doodling on a pad of paper.

His personal secretary, Ann, knocked on his door. After a moment, he told her to come in and sit down.

Ann sat in the armchair before his desk, "Having a bad day?"

"No, I was thinking of my son, William. I need to do something about his situation, but I have no idea what."

Ann sat quietly and then said apprehensively, "Have you talked to him lately?"

"No, I haven't. I don't know if I'm embarrassed or disgusted with William."

Ann thought about what he said. She didn't know if she should continue that conversation but decided to go ahead, "Aaron, can I put in my two cents?"

"Of course, you can. I need help."

She wiped her brow and proceeded, "Up to now, you were very guarded about any conversation about William. This may be hard to hear, but you have got to put this to rest. You have to forgive him, not forget what he did, but forgive him. The hardest part of forgiveness is taking the first step. Go to him. There's nothing you can do about the situation he got himself into. William needs his father to be a dad, not a judge."

Aaron wiped tears from his eyes, "How did you get so wise. Maybe you should be the one sitting here in my chair. What you have asked me to do is hard. But you are right. I'll set up a meeting with him today."

"Can I record what you said?"

"You mean about calling for a meeting today?"

"No, the part about me being right."

"Get out of here," Aaron said, laughing and wiping his eyes.

Conrad went to Rod's office and told Rod the sequence of events in the conference room and the second interview person when the cops took that guy to jail.

They laughed well, then Rod said, "Well, is that guy still here?"

"Yeah, he's in the conference room. Come on."

Rod said as they entered the room, "I'm glad you stayed after what you saw coming in the door."

Larry stood and shook hands with Rod, "You all had me worried for a while. I've seen my share of handcuffed subjects to last a lifetime."

"Nice to meet you. Could you tell us a little about yourself? You have a great résumé, so you can skip that unless you want to tell us anything else."

"My name is Larry Groves. I'm 54 years old and married to my fabulous wife, Louise. We have three children and seven grandchildren – Do you want to see pictures?" As he reached for his wallet. "As you've seen in my résumé, I've been with the Seattle PD for twenty years. The last five years as a detective."

Conrad asked, "What brings you to Monterey?"

Larry sipped water, "Honestly, I've had enough of a big city. I'm sure you know police officers don't get the respect we used to. I traveled through this area on Highway One and told my wife I wanted to move here when I retired. So, a month ago we moved here. Empty nest."

Rod had a questioning look and asked, "But why back into detective mode?"

"That's easy to answer. I love the work."

Rod looked at Conrad, "Conrad, do the honors."

A big smile came over his face, and he slid over a couple of sheets containing the salary and benefits, "If you agree to what's on those sheets. Let me be the first to say welcome to the Carson Detective Agency."

All three stood and shook hands after Larry Groves said yes to Conrad and Rod.

Rod said to Larry, "Come into my office. There is something I need to tell you."

As they settled in Rod's office, Rod began, "Larry, it's only fair that I tell you about me. A couple of weeks ago, I was diagnosed with Parkinson's. Conrad is now our Executive VP and will be doing more and more. I still try to do what needs to be done, but as you might have seen, my hand tremors and gait aren't what they used to be. We have also hired a new administrative person to take Sue's place when she leaves to get married. Conrad and I will be here at least next week to help you settle. I told Monique Cole to start Monday. You can start then also if you're ready."

"If it's okay with you, I would love to come in tomorrow and start to set up everything, so I'll be ready to go by

Monday."

"That's fine with me. See you tomorrow."

Terminal Island, Federal Correctional Institution, is in San Pedro, California. Aaron was approaching the prison but had to pull off the road. His heart was racing, and his mind was full of doubts. Would William even see him? Was he angry and depressed?

Aaron's thoughts turned to a silent prayer: *Lord, you know my heart. I want to be a dad to Bill today. God, you have to help me. I need your strength.*

Aaron checked in with the authorities and waited in the vehicle waiting area until he received a call to enter the prison. Aaron tried to keep his thoughts on positive things, but his head was full of doubt.

The call came in that he could enter.

He was checked out and entered a room where his son was sitting. Of course, a guard was at the door.

William Sterling stood, "Hi, Dad. I would give you a hug, but they said no touching."

Aaron sat and looked at Bill intently, "I don't know what to say."

"That's a first. I never saw you when you didn't have something to say."

"I know, Bill. It's so good to see you. I need to tell you so much. Ann said some things the other day that shook me to my feet. She said I needed to see, forgive, love, and listen to you. I'm sorry I've not come sooner."

"I'm the one who is sorry. Thank you for forgiving me. I needed that. I was so ashamed that it was hard to even look at you. What I did was wrong. I tried to justify my actions, but realizing they were selfish didn't take long."

Aaron also realized his doubts were unfounded: "How are you doing?"

"I had a better frame of mind once I forgave myself. How are you doing?"

"That's one of the reasons I wanted to come to see you. Remember Sue, who helped me when this whole thing started. We have been dating, and I have asked her to marry me. What are your thoughts on that?"

"Believe it or not, since I was sentenced and sent here, I have thought you needed to get married. Mom would agree, and I do, also. James has been by and hinted that you might be getting serious with someone."

"James visited you? I didn't know that. It's like your older brother to keep tabs on you."

Aaron and Bill talked until the time was up to leave.

"Just to let you know, Bill, we are trying to release you from here, but it takes time. Don't give up."

"I won't, Dad. I love you." Bill said as he turned so that Aaron and the guard did not see the tear in his eyes.

Aaron's walk back to his car was quickened and more contented. *Ann was right!*

CHAPTER FOURTEEN

The first two-thirds of travel between San Jose and Napa Valley was mundane. The highway gently ascends under a canopy of trees. It spills out into a beautiful valley filled with vineyards and ranches.

They boast the world's premier wine regions of over four hundred wineries. Some of the best hotels and resorts dot the landscape around Napa. Whatever you like to do, the end result is something exceptional.

Conrad was driving Rod's convertible Corvette. Rod put his seat back to take in the scenes and the beautiful summer sky. The mission of their trip was to see Cindy and learn more about her brother, Clint, and his possible entrance to Med School.

Rod gave Cindy a call when they were close to the Royston Estate. It was one of California's most stunning estates, if not *the* most prominent.

Cindy waved as they drove in the circular driveway.

"Hi, guys. I see you enjoyed the ride up here today. Conrad, are you going to take me for a ride later?"

Rod sputtered but spoke unsteadily, "Hey, wait a minute. I'll take you for a ride, or better yet, you can drive."

Cindy laughed, "That's okay with me. You have enough insurance?"

Conrad replied, "He's got lots of insurance. But we don't want him in the hospital again."

"Cindy knows how much I love hospitals, don't you, hon?"

Cindy laughed, "Conrad, don't get Rod started on hospitals. When I picked him up from the hospital, he must have complained for around two hours."

"Cindy, you're exaggerating again. It was only one and a half hours."

They all snickered as they headed for the door.

They walked into the home, and Cindy guided them to their sprawling family room.

Cindy offered refreshments, and they sat down and enjoyed the next hour catching up on things and simply relaxing.

"Is Clint here, Cindy?" Rod asked.

"Yep, I'll go get him. I'm sure he's anxious to tell you what happened since we last talked."

A few minutes later, a smiling Clint entered the room with his arm around his sister.

Rod responded, "You sure look a lot better, Clint. Okay, out with the news."

Clint could hardly keep his excitement under control, "Yesterday, I received a letter from UC Davis School of Medicine. I start Med School in the fall."

They all clapped and stood, and Clint came over and hugged Rod, "Thank you, Rod. Without your help and support, this would not be possible. At the earliest time, I will go to San Jose to express my thanks to Susan. After all, her suggestion helped UC Davis to accept me."

Rod spoke, "I won't spoil the news for Susan. Don't wait

too long. I'm not good at keeping secrets."

The end of their hike down the eastern mountain trail into the foothills to the trailhead was much easier than the higher areas. With their suspect in front, Josh and David put handcuffs on Derik. The rope tied to his waist wasn't needed on reasonably flat ground. David had called the local Sheriff's Department to have a deputy at the trailhead to take Derik into custody.

They saw two large Inyo County Sheriff's Deputies at the end of their non-pleasant hiking excursion.

Josh told David, "Those are the biggest Sheriff Deputy officers I have ever seen."

Derik said under his breath but loud enough for Josh and David to hear, "Oh, No."

"If I were you, Derik, I would keep my mouth shut and don't do anything rash," David responded.

When the deputies searched Derik and placed their handcuffs on him, they sat him in one of Inyo County's vehicles. The deputies, Josh and David, shot the breeze for a while. The deputies might have been huge, but they were enjoyable.

One of the Sheriff's deputies asked, "What did you say to him to make him so calm."

Josh said, "Look in the mirror, and you'll know the answer."

The other deputy told them Fresno County deputies would meet us halfway so we didn't have to go all the way around the mountains.

Fresno County Sheriff's Department men transferred Derik to their marked vehicle hours later. Derik was in no mood to talk, so Josh sat in the back seat to get some sleep.

Another Fresno County deputy transported the two Park Rangers back to the trailhead at Roads End. On the trip to Fresno, Josh and David discovered that Marcus and Javier were up in the mountains doing some sightseeing.

Josh said, "We do all the work, and they are up there having fun. What a life."

Dollar Lake in the early sunlit morning was something to behold. The sun peeked around the eastern cliffs about a quarter of a mile from the lake. The deep shadows from the nearby trees were casting their spell mixed with the sparkling sunlight coming off the lake. A trout or two occasionally jumped, making far-reaching ripples that fan out in ever-lengthening circles.

Javier was on a boulder that sat chair height along the shoreline. Occasionally, he would grunt or say, "Oh," as he half lay on the big rock.

Marcus started to make breakfast, "Hey, man, you want something to eat, or are you going to stay there all day?"

"I'm hungry, but I could stay here all day."

Marcus responded, "Okay, I'm starving, so I'll enjoy eating all this food."

Javier jumped up, "No, you don't. I'm coming, *I'm coming*." He said as he bounded up the hill where the camp was located.

"You know what, Marcus? If I had the means and a way to survive here, I might just stay until Winter."

"No, Javier, you wouldn't last a week. You enjoy food too much. Remember those great restaurants in Fresno?"

"Oh, but look at all this around us. Wouldn't you like to stay also?"

"Maybe for a day or two, but I like people in my life. I

mean, you're okay, but more people around."

As they ate, they kept looking around at the beauty surrounding them.

With a mouth full of food, Marcus said, "How about we check a little more of the area today, and tomorrow we'll head back to the Castle Domes. I would like to see what it's like on the other side of the Domes."

Javier responded, "Sounds like a plan, man. Early tomorrow, we'll pack up our gear and head out."

David and Josh sat around a desk in one of the Fresno PD's offices and began writing their report. After about an hour, they called the Carson Detective Agency in San Jose to talk to Conrad about their report. David told Conrad that an electronic account was already sent to Susan, the Administrative Manager.

Conrad asked, "Thanks. Have you heard from Javier and Marcus?"

"Yes, just before we reached Fresno, the Fresno County deputies told us they were up in the mountains having fun."

Conrad laughed, "Having fun? We don't pay employees to have fun. Well, you all deserve it. Why don't you take a few days off before returning here."

"Thanks, Conrad. I think I will sit in on the interview with Derik Thomson. I'd like to hear what happened at Kings Canyon National Park."

The Royston home was a buzz of activity, preparing for a big dinner occasion. They were hosting three older couples their age. One of the couples was bringing their son, a single adult. Cindy's mom and the house staff pitched in to create a memorable dinner party. Finally, Cindy pulled her mother aside so they could get dressed.

"Mom, let the staff help take care of the kitchen meal while we get dressed. After that, we can go around and see if everything is in place," Cindy said as she took her mother's arm.

"But there is so much to do."

"It's okay, Mom. They can get everything done in plenty of time."

Clinton Senior arrived home late morning from Washington, D.C., with his bodyguard. His son Clint and he had a long conversation in the Senior's office that afternoon. They were very close since Clint spent a few months in prison. A few years back, Clint had concocted a plot to get a lot of money from his dad through a poorly thought-out plan.

When Cindy walked in, Clint and his dad almost forgot about the big dinner.

"Okay, you guys, you're not wearing that to our dinner, are you?"

Clinton said, "No, my daughter, we'll head upstairs and get dressed. This is a formal affair, isn't it?"

"Yes, Father. Now get going."

The Roystons had set the dinner time for six, so the party could relax in the formal living room. Drinks and hors d'oeuvres were served by the extra help they had hired for the evening.

Soon the room was busy with laughter and snacking.

The one couple with their son was a little late. The doorbell rang, and the butler opened the door for them.

Cindy has in the kitchen making sure the dinner meal

was ready. She headed back toward the living room. As she left the kitchen, she turned back toward the kitchen, saying something, and banged into someone.

She was embarrassed and didn't see who it was until she looked up at the good-looking guy with blond hair.

In shock, she finally recognized Cory, the man she had encountered coming out of a store.

"What are you doing here?" Cindy asked.

"I was invited. What are you doing here?" Cory said.

"You are the Walters's son?"

"And you must be Cindy Ralston?" Cory said as he began to laugh.

"Cory Walters, welcome to the Royston home," Cindy said cautiously.

Cory's folks were still standing there quizzically, looking at Cory and Cindy. They asked how Cindy and Cory knew each other.

Cory chuckled, "You're not going to believe it. This is the beautiful gal I ran into this morning going into a store. I didn't get Cindy's last name, and I thought I would never run into her again – no pun intended."

Cindy escorted the Walters into the living room. Everyone knew the Walters, but they didn't know Cory. He attended UCLA. After college, he joined the service and recently got out. Introductions were made, and Cindy advised them that dinner would be served in ten minutes.

The seven guests and the Roystons enjoyed dinner time and the drinks after the meal.

Cory stole several looks at Cindy during the meal. Cindy caught one glimpse, and it remained for some time.

Cindy thought; he *sure is good-looking.*

After dinner, all the guests and the Roystons headed for the large living room. On the way, Cory asked Cindy for a stroll around the home and flower garden. Of course, they continued laughing about bumping into each other and not knowing they would see each other so soon.

Cory was a real gentleman, and they talked for a long time. The party broke up when they walked back into the home, and everyone was saying their goodbyes.

Cindy walked the Walters out to their car.

Cory looked at Cindy, "I would like to see you again. Could we have lunch sometime?"

"Sure, I'd like that."

When their vehicle left, Cindy realized she had a dilemma brewing. What about Rod?

Juan Garcia had many questions concerning the Al Fletcher case. He may have some answers soon.

Guards brought Derik into an interrogation room. Juan would let him stew in there for a while. That should soften Derik up so that he would talk.

Fifteen minutes later, Juan and David entered the interview room and sat facing Derik. Juan turned on the recorder and then gave Derik his rights. Derik did not like sitting there, and his nervousness began to show. He drank more water.

Juan started by asking Derik about his drug habit and the drugs on him when he was captured by David and Josh.

"Yeah, I do some drugs. I didn't do anything else."

"I didn't ask about anything else. What else went on in the mountains?"

"Nothing happened. You're just trying to confuse me. Okay, I had some drugs on me."

"Do you know Al Fletcher?"

"No, I don't know him. Who is he?"

"He's dead. Now, do you know him?"

"You can't pin that on me. I have never killed anyone."

Juan looked at Derik hard, "We have witnesses that say you knew Al Fletcher well. What was the fight about?"

"Okay, I knew him. I thought he was a phony. He tried to get me to quit drugs. I may have a problem with drugs. But I'm not addicted, and I didn't kill him."

"Didn't you see him on the Baxter Lake Trail?"

"No."

Derik said, "Okay, I saw him but didn't kill him."

Juan questioned Derik for over an hour. Josh and Jada were watching on close-circuit TV and thought he would crack. He didn't. Derik denied the murder.

Juan walked out and told Josh and Jada, "We must review the crime scene photos and the physical evidence to make this case stick. This may be a long, hard case to solve."

Juan reflected on the interrogation with Derik. Juan realized that he did not say Al Fletcher was murdered. Why did Derik say he didn't kill him?

CHAPTER FIFTEEN

Jason Marrone contacted Conrad. Jason and Ryan wanted to meet with Conrad and Rod about the building the detective agency was in. Conrad went to Rod's office to discuss the possibilities.

Rod looked up as Conrad came in and sat down, "I'm not sure we can know what they're up to. So let's wait until they get here. No worries."

"I know, not to worry, but it could be anything. Bad or good," Conrad countered.

"What time are they arriving?"

"In twenty minutes. Ten o'clock. You want to meet here or in the conference room."

Rod responded, "Let's meet here. It's big enough."

"Okay, I'll bring them in when they get here."

Conrad left, and Rod put his paperwork away and took out a pad of paper to write on. No telling what they wanted.

A short time later, Conrad escorted Jason and Ryan into Rod's office.

Rod came around his desk with his hand, "Hi there, let's sit at the conference table."

"What brings you by today, "Rod said.

Jason cleared his throat, "Ryan and I have been talking a lot this week. Does the Carson Detective Agency want to buy this building? Ryan and I agree that we want to sell this building. As you know, I am in the real estate business and have a fairly good idea of what it will go for. My wife and I will move from our apartment into Dad's home. This will help our family a lot. Ryan likes where he's at because it's closer to his company. Are you interested?"

Rod looked at Conrad, "Conrad and I have also been discussing this same subject. I can say we are interested. I have also talked to our banker and attorney. It will depend on what you want for it."

Ryan responded, "That's a hard number to pin down. The market is so flexible these days. What is fair this week may not be fair next week. After I overcame my selfishness after Dad died, I returned to earth. We want to be reasonable."

Jason said, "We have looked at fair numbers, but in this case, we will be lowering the cost."

Rod was delighted, "You both have made us very happy with your presentation. But we also want to be fair. Is it alright to call you a week after discussing it and crunching numbers?"

Jason replied, "If Dad was still here, he would be gratified with this conversation. Don't hurry; call me when you want to talk about it."

Ryan said, "We need to leave. Looking forward to our next meeting.

Rod and Conrad stayed in Rod's office.

"Well, what did you think of that, Rod? I was nervous for nothing."

"Relax, buddy, there will be more times like this. Rod

said as he went behind his desk.

Conrad replied, "Just to let you know, since we last talked about owning this building, I notified some people I know about renting an office or two. Many were very excited about renting here if we owned the building. I don't think it would be long before we could fill each room."

Rod responded, "Time will tell. *Time will tell.*"

Jada received a call from Juan Garcia. "Jada, want to go out again this evening?"

"Sure, doing some shopping now. What Time?"

"Let's start a little earlier this time, around five. We'll have a great dinner, then I have a surprise for you."

"What's the surprise?" She said excitedly.

"It wouldn't be a surprise if I told you, would it?"

"I'll just have to wait. I don't like postponements. See you at five.

"Okay, see you later."

"Oh, is it casual or dress-up?"

"Casual, Please. Bye."

Joe Brooks called Rod, "Are you busy? I have to talk to you."

"You can come over anytime, or do you want me to come to your home."

"No, Rod, I'll come over. I need to get away. I have some questions for you and Conrad. I will be there in twenty minutes, okay?"

"No problem, come on over. See you soon."

Rod left his office to get more coffee and stopped by Conrad's office.

"Busy?"

"No, why?"

"Joe Brooks called and wanted to come over and talk to us to ask some questions."

"Okay, your office?"

"Yes. I'm sure it's about Joe's boy, Roger. We'll see what he wants soon enough."

About ten minutes later, Conrad wandered into Rod's office and sat in the corner seating area. He set his coffee cup on the coffee table, "I told Susan to bring him in here."

It wasn't long before Susan arrived at Rod's office with Joe.

Joe started the conversation, "Thanks for letting me come over on such short notice. I just had to get away from home for a while. How have you guys been doing?"

Conrad replied, "Come on over and sit down. We are okay, just busy. Did Susan offer you something to drink?"

"Of course I did. What kind of an Admin person do you think I am, Conrad?" Susan said as she exited the door.

Rod said, "How can we help you, Joe?"

"My wife, Dawn, is on the warpath. She told me to get out of her hair, so I started doing legal work. Now, she's mad at me because I don't care about Roger. After all, I'm working now. Guys, never get married. The Library of Congress could not contain the books needed to figure out a woman."

Rod smiled, and Conrad laughed, "You ought to have heard the conversation that Rod and I had come up from Monterey. I was telling Rod that I needed to find a girlfriend."

Joe said, "You've got one right out there," pointing to

the outer offices. Susan is a winner."

"I thought you needed to ask us some questions, Joe," Rod said seriously.

Joe said, "Guys, how long does it take to find a missing person. It's been weeks since Roger went missing. This wait with no answers is tough on our family. Any word yet?"

Rod responded, "Joe, we have no idea what it's like to have a family member missing. I must walk in your shoes to understand the pain and misery. Conrad did receive a call from our detectives in the Fresno area. Conrad, tell him what they told you."

"They didn't have a lot to tell. Absolutely, no sign of Roger. There are hundreds of square miles in those mountains. No one has any idea where he went or where he is. The body, the Kings Canyon National Park Rangers, found was identified as Al or Albert Fletcher. He is from Fresno and is co-owner of a fitness club in Fresno. His co-owner has not been found either."

Conrad breathed deeply and continued, "Two other detectives of ours took a man into custody for things he did to his so-called girlfriend. Fresno PD interrogated him. Derik Thomson is also from the Fresno area. He's a drug addict and a tough guy. So far, they have not charged Derik Thomson with Al's murder. While all that was happening, numerous search parties were looking for Al's co-owner and Roger. Joe, we'll find him."

Joe took all that in and replied, "I know your detectives and so many other people are looking for him. The area he went to is huge, and you're right; he could be anywhere. Do me one favor, if you would."

Rod replied, "Just name it, Joe. If it's within our power to do so, we will. What is it?"

"If it turns out bad. I mean, if Roger is dead, then call me on my cell phone. Give it a call sign, like 'got it,' so if I'm home, I can call you back outside."

Conrad said, "Roger will be found; he's only lost. The worse is that he's injured and can't get around much. That's all, Joe. Don't have those negative thoughts."

"I hear you, but it's hard not to have those thoughts run through my head. I'll try, guys. Thank you for your concern, and tell your detectives I am grateful for their hard work."

After Joe left, Rod and Conrad talked more about the case and how hard it was on Joe and his family.

Rod said, "I hope you or I never see the day when someone we love goes missing. I look at Joe and his family and wouldn't wish that on anyone."

Conrad said, "A cousin of mine had his young daughter go missing after school. Four days later, a road crew looked under a tarp beside the road. She was dead under that canvas."

Rod reflected on what Conrad had said, "We don't think it would happen to us. I mean, we keep on going through life, not thinking about bad things. Then one day…" Rod's voice trailed off.

"My cousin's family fell apart. They soon got a divorce. He's been lost ever since. Not missing, just out there, not thinking right now."

"Conrad, I've got to get back to work. Let's not talk about bad things. We need to have a good attitude and not get ourselves down.

Juan's evening with Jada went so well. He took her to the best Mexican Restaurant in Fresno. His mother's home.

Jada was a little apprehensive about going to his mom's home, but what could anything wrong happen. They pulled in front of a small but well-kept brown stucco home. Beautiful well-managed flowers and plants dotted her landscaped yard. It was apparent to Jada that Juan was very proud of his mother and her home.

Jada started to open her car door, and Juan stopped her. He said, "Wait a minute, I'll get your car door."

Jada didn't know what to say, but she waited.

Juan opened her door and held his hand out to help her from the car. She couldn't talk for a moment.

She stopped Juan, "Juan, I have never had a man help me like you. In my culture, you just had to fend for yourself."

Just before they went in, Jada said, "I'm afraid."

"Haven't you been in a home before?"

"Of course I have. I mean, meeting your mother. I'm African American."

"Yes, I know, and I'm Mexican. My mother knows about you. Just be yourself, and everything will go fine."

Jada was greeted by an older, overweight sweet lady. She didn't look funny at Jada at all. Rosa Garcia started asking Jada questions until Juan suggested her food was getting cold. Rosa took the hint and went back into the kitchen. Juan lived in that home before he left after high school. He showed Jada around and then to the dining room.

He pulled her chair back for her to sit. Jada was taking in all that Juan did for her. She had never experienced this kind of treatment before. Her dad was a drunkard, and so was her first husband. After her divorce, she vowed she would never marry again. But she could get used to this kind of care.

When they were all seated, Rosa grabbed her left hand, and Juan held onto her right hand. Rosa and Juan bowed their heads; Rosa started her prayer, "Lord, we are grateful that Jada is joining us for our meal." Jada looked around.

Rosa continued, "Lord, would you bless this food to our bodies to help us grow and serve you more."

Jada waited and kept her eyes closed until Juan spoke, "You can open your eyes now. We're ready to eat a delicious meal."

Jada was embarrassed because she had never heard anyone pray except in church once a year at Christmas.

Rosa started bringing out the food. All traditional Mexican food. Jada ate at a Mexican restaurant only a couple of times. She thought, *do I use the regular fork, knife, and spoon-like ordinary people?* She was relieved when Juan picked up his fork.

Rosa had prepared a traditional Mexican dinner. Chile Rellenos, Tostadas, Enchiladas, some with red sauce and a few with white sauce. Chips with Mole sauce and a beautiful multi-colored Gelatina De Mosaico (Mosaic Jell-O).

Jada decided as she watched Rosa and Juan to not take as much as they did, so she took a little of each item.

Jada finally took her first bite, "Ummm, that's good." It didn't take her long to finish the small amount of food on her plate, "May I have some more?"

"Of course, you can. " Rosa said, "Have you not had Mexican food before."

"Yes, a few times at a restaurant, but it was not like this. Thank you for preparing this delicious meal."

Rosa smiled, "You're welcome. It's a joy to have you join

us tonight. Tell me a little about yourself."

Jada talked between bites and told Rosa her background.

"I went to a community college where I majored in Computer Science. I absolutely love computers and what you can do with them. I did not have a perfect home life, so I left as soon as possible. Coming from South LA can make a person tougher and more streetwise. I did odd jobs until I joined a small detective agency in LA. I put my resumé out, and Rod Carson of the Carson Detective Agency hired me not long ago."

Rosa got up and started for her kitchen, "Dessert coming right up."

Jada responded, "Not for me, I'm -------." She glanced over to Juan shaking his head no.

"I would love to have some dessert," Jada lied.

From the kitchen, "Juan, you can stop shaking your head no, now."

Juan and Jada laughed as quietly as they could. From the kitchen, they heard a guffaw.

Rosa brought out the dessert. A Mexican Flan with caramel drizzled on top. Jada's first bite was small. She sat back with the most satisfying look.

"So good, it's like crème brûlée.

CHAPTER SIXTEEN

Rod woke up shaking all over. What's happening? He decided to lay there until the fog went away. Rod closed his eyes for some time, but the shaking didn't stop. Not today! *This is the Neurologist appointment day. Cindy will be here soon. She can't see me this way. What if I can't get up? She'll have to dress me.*

Rod almost fainted at that thought. Oh, well, I might like that.

Rod laughed and got up very slowly. The shaking had subsided, and he made it to the bathroom.

While in the bathroom, Rod heard the front door shut, "Are you decent?"

"No, could you shut my bedroom door and make yourself comfortable."

"You want me to make myself comfortable in your bedroom?"

"Shut my bedroom door and make yourself comfortable *in the living room.*"

Cindy chuckled and did as he wanted. She entered the kitchen and found he didn't wash his dishes last night. She heard the shower come on, so knowing it would be some time, she pulled out her Surface Go 3 tablet and continued reading one of the books.

Rod almost fell a couple of times in the shower. He had

some grab bars installed, so he grabbed one of them.

Rod thought again; *this would be worst for her than just helping put my clothes on*. He laughed at that.

He had found out it took longer to shower and get his clothes on. *What does the future hold?*

Cindy was finishing another chapter of her book when Rod emerged from his bedroom.

"I'm having more problems lately," Rod said.

Cindy looked up at him, "You sure are. Maybe you should zip up now."

Rod turned away from her and zipped up. How embarrassing.

Cindy decided she better not laugh, "There, all better. Tell me, what's going on lately with your Parkinson's?"

Rod turned back to Cindy as though nothing had happened, "I'm beginning to shake all over. It may not be all over, but it feels like that. Stumbling, tremors, and other things I won't mention. Cindy, I don't know what the future holds for us."

A tear came to her eye. She brushed it away.

Cindy turned to Rod, "We may have more answers today at your appointment. We should be leaving; I don't know how the traffic flow will get to Oakland."

"I'll get my sweater in case it's cooler in the doctor's office."

Cindy knew her way around San Francisco and Oakland. She started on the I-880 N and had to stitch to the I-580. The trip would take about an hour, depending on traffic. Rod found some easy-listening music on the radio and sat back to try to enjoy the ride.

"I'm very nervous about this appointment," Rod said finally, "I know I am having more and more symptoms lately. This Parkinson's is beginning to scare me, and I worry about you and how this will affect you."

"Don't worry about me. I'm okay. Let's talk about something else. What are your plans for the rest of the week?"

"I'm very anxious for Joe Brooks. There are a lot of people in the mountains looking for Roger. Joe and especially his wife Dawn are not doing well. I can't know how they feel, but I can empathize with the Brooks family. I can't know how it feels unless I walk in their shoes. What would possess a guy to tell his folks that he will only be gone a week and even tell them which trail he was going on."

"That does sound strange."

Rod continued, "The Park Rangers and our people have been through that trail without anyone seeing him. By now, he must have gone somewhere else and got lost. Who knows? It will be good to have our detectives home. We need them. Conrad, Eva, and Jerry are doing their best to keep up with business, but it's getting hectic. We are growing our business, and I can't even help. It's frustrating."

Cindy said, "You've got some wonderful people. The best detectives and administrative help around. Trust, encourage, and love them. They will fight a raging fire for you when you do that."

"Thanks, Cindy, that means a lot. I need to do more of those things. Tell me about your week?"

"Oh, the funniest thing happened yesterday. I was out shopping in San Jose and in a store. When I got through shopping, I was carrying some packages out the door and ran right into a man, not watching what I was doing. Packages all over the place. We both bent down and bumped heads. What was even more embarrassing was he was a handsome blond-headed man."

"Should I begin to get worried about this guy?"

"Wait, you haven't heard the best part. You remember we had a huge dinner with three other couples. Well, one of the couples brought their son along. I knew the Walters but never met their son."

"No, you're telling me he was the one you bumped into?"

"Yes, I bump into him again at our house. You know me, I was talking to someone else and not watching where I was going. He is very nice and gentlemanly. Oh, and did I tell you how good-looking he is?"

"Now I *am* getting worried."

"I better tell you the whole story. After dinner, Cory wanted to go for a walk around our home. When we went inside, the couples were getting ready to leave. So, I walked them to their vehicles. At the last moment, he asked me if he and I could have lunch or dinner. Before he got in their car, I said sure, and then they drove off. I think I have a problem."

"I should be mad, but I'm not. Many things are happening now, and I don't know the future. I think it's a good thing for a dinner date. Why not? You may find out he's a zero and I'm a ten. I think you should work out your feelings and think about the future. If you don't, you might regret our relationship."

Cindy dabbed her eyes with a tissue, "How did you get so wise? It must have been your mom and dad. I care for you a lot. You may be right. I should know my feelings and work out any distractions. Thank you, Rod."

Rod was not happy about the last conversation. However, he knew he cared for her. Nothing is worse in a relationship than to have one who regrets their decision

to make sure the connection is solid. Still, it's hard to watch the other person have doubts about the future.

The neurologist's office was bright but lacking in comfort. The chairs were elegant but hard as stone. Maybe they wanted patients to consider their uncomfortableness instead of their medical problems. The pictures on the wall were typically ultra-modern, with lines and circles that made no sense. What's worse is the doctor is never on time. Rod was sure they were busy doing whatever doctors did when they didn't want to see another patient with many problems.

Rod didn't want to be cynical, but it's his nature to question everything. That's what makes a good detective.

Twenty-five minutes after the appointment time, a nurse with a nurse smile came out to escort Rod and Cindy to the small *interrogation* room. At least, that's what Rod would call it. Someone would ask about this, leading to a follow-up question, etc.

Rod knew this room would be another waiting room until the doctor decided to make his grand entrance.

Doctor J. A. Willow entered Rod and Cindy's room a few minutes later. Rod saw her and thought, *J.A., Just a willow.* He smiled broadly to hide his thinking and said pleasantly, "Good morning Doctor Willow."

"What brings you in today?" She spoke.

Rod had another thought which he didn't express out loud, *that must be covered in med school 101. What brings you in today?*

Rod regained his composure and told the doctor that he had been diagnosed with Parkinson's by his personal doctor. Rod related that the symptoms seemed to be getting worse. The tremors, staggered gait, headaches, and bladder problems created mental doubts and fears.

Doctor Willow followed up by asking additional questions about his movements and muscle rigidity. She was very businesslike but pleasant.

Rod began to feel bad about his earlier thoughts.

The doctor did some further tests. Standing to see balance, she had Rod walk across the room and back. She asked some questions, and Rod wished Cindy was not in the room. Doc Willow wrote a bunch of notes on the computer in the room. This process took thirty-five minutes.

When she was finished asking questions, the doctor said, "You have the symptoms of Parkinson's, but there are, on rare occasions, other disorders that can cause Parkinson's disease symptoms. In your case, I think it is Parkinson's, but there is a procedure I would like to do that would tell us without a doubt what you have. I want you in our hospital for brain scans, physical examination, and lumbar puncture."

Cindy winched when the doctor said the last thing.

Rod said, "What's a limber puncture?"

The doctor smiled, "No, it's lumbar puncture – a spinal tap."

Rod responded, "Oh, that sounds painful."

"No, they will deaden the skin where they put the needle in the lumbar region of your lower back. They collect cerebrospinal fluid, so we can test to find out what you have. Hardly any pain, but you may have headaches for a couple of days. We should have the test results in three days. I will call you with the results. You can go home this afternoon if everything goes well with your tests."

Rod has yet to determine if he feels better or not.

Cindy said, "Thank you, Doctor Willow.

"The hospital is down the street. My nurse will give you the address, Mrs. Carson."

"Oh, I'm not Mrs. Carson. Maybe someday. But we're very close friends."

"We should have established that before you came in, but he needs support. Good friends need good friends."

And the doctor was gone. Waiting again for the nurse.

The hospital was in the same décor as the doctor's office, except for much longer halls and more comfortable chairs. At the information desk sat a tried security officer who suggested Rod take a wheelchair. Rod did not argue because he was already fatigued from the doctor's office visit. Cindy said she would push him wherever they needed to go.

Cindy took Rod to the neurological section of the hospital. Three floors and two long corridors later, they arrived.

Another waiting room with the same smell and decorations. The pictures were nondescript scenes of mountains and meadows.

This time a non-smiling nurse came to get Rod. Cindy could not go with him. Rod was wheeled out the door to get some brain scans.

It was good that Rod was not claustrophobic because that scanner would send anyone claustrophobic into a suffocating experience.

Rod felt they couldn't find his brain because it took so long to locate it. After an exhausting 30 minutes, they took Rod back to the waiting room with Cindy. She took one look at him and decided not to say a word. He just sat there, staring off into space.

After a few minutes, Rod turned to Cindy, "Don't ever get a scan. It will drive you stark raving mad."

Cindy just shook her head yes, and still kept her mouth shut.

At long last, She said, "That bad, huh?"

"Yep."

Blood work was done. Then the same unsmiling nurse entered the waiting room, "Rod Carson?"

Under his breath, Rod mumbled, *The same darn nurse that came to get me forty-five minutes ago can't remember who I am.*

"Shush," Cindy whispered.

"I'm Rod Carson," Rod said super sweetly.

Cindy gave him one of her unique *good* looks.

This time Rod was in for a treat. Lay on your stomach, don't move. This won't hurt. The worse part was that cold liquid they put on the small of your back to clean the area where the needle goes in. They must keep that stuff in a freezer somewhere.

After the procedure, Rod was all smiles because it was not terrible. He almost felt bad about the thoughts he had.

The same nurse took Rod back to the waiting room.

"Remain here, Mr. Carlyle, until we tell you, you can go."

Rod didn't even correct her with the right name.

A guy across the waiting room said, "She got your name wrong, didn't she?"

CHAPTER SEVENTEEN

The following morning Rod, Conrad, and Susan spent a few hours looking throughout their office building. Conrad had connected with a reputable building contractor to conduct a thorough inspection. At least six people from that firm were checking the building from the top, the roof, and the bottom. Conrad also had a Real Estate group that specialized in office buildings to give a quote on what the building was worth.

After the different groups had completed inspections of the building, the head person of each group met with Ron and Conrad in their large Conference room.

The building contractor went through extensive files on each area of the building. He gave his opinion on the pros and cons of each area of the building. He also had facts and figures about the whole building and every office. His conclusion on the size of the building was 17,800 square feet. Some offices were the same size approximately. Two-thirds of the offices were of different sizes. His opinion of the building overall was excellent. He also noted that the building was built in 2000.

Next, the Real Estate head person gave her quotes. "This building is in perfect shape. The street optics are outstanding. What I am quoting is the price of this size of establishment. The cost varies depending on the location.

This building will sell for between seven point five million to almost nine million. It would go for between eight million and eight point five million.

Rod thanked the groups for their insightful and complete inspection analysis. Susan came and escorted them out.

Conrad went with Rod to Rod's office. Conrad spoke first, "Well, what did you think?"

Rod sat back on his chair and sipped his soft drink, "I've been looking online for the cost of buildings in this area. Actually, what she quoted was in line with other buildings like ours. It was good to hear that there were no major issues and everything was in good shape."

Conrad said, "I also have checked with some of my real estate friends, and this quote was what they thought also. Now what?"

"Let me contact the company's financial advisor and attorney. We need their input before we can continue. Let's see, it's mid-afternoon. Why don't you call your accountant and see what he says about buying this building? How about you pick me up at eight in the morning? We'll do breakfast, then visit my office to see where we stand. I feel good about the purchase, but we must crunch numbers."

"I agree with you. Did you forget I have to take you home? Let me know when you are ready to leave for the day."

"Yes, I did forget. Okay, partner, see you in a while."

Aaron sat in his office atop his mid-size, high-rise

building. He was doing some heavy thinking. He had turned his chair to look out a huge window.

Ann walked by his office and then came back to knock on his open door, "You look like you were out there somewhere," As she pointed out the window.

"Yes, I was. Come in and sit down. I have something to ask you,"

Ann came and sat in an armchair that was by the window.

"Ann, you're a sagacious person. I'm fortunate to have you as a right-hand woman to work beside me."

Ann looked at him with a funny face, "Okay, what did I do this time?"

Aaron laughed, "No, you *are* wise. You helped me see the way I was treating William. You were extremely correct. I mean what you said to me. Thank you."

"I feel better, I think."

"Ann, I've been thinking about William's brother, James. I know he was wrong for not telling me about William's conspiracy about the embezzlement. I'm really not sure how much James knew about it. I love both my sons' equality. How do I mend or build back the fence once it's broken."

"What I would say, Aaron, is the same thing I told you about William. Forgive, listen, and love him. You might find a whole different fence that wasn't broken.

It became hushed in Aaron's office.

Finally, Aaron spoke, staring out the window, "Ann, the older I get, the more tender I find myself. I'll do it. I'll call James right away and set up a meeting."

"Remember," Ann said, "This won't be an employee meeting. Not here. Go where you think he would like."

"Great advice. Thank you again. I must give you a

raise."

Ann snickered as she left Aaron's office.

Conrad was a little early to pick up Rod. This day could be a big time for the Carson Detective Agency. Rod was not as excited as Conrad because of his Parkinson's. His sleep was on and off during the night.

Conrad was sitting in the living room when he shouted, "Need any help, Ron?"

"No, I'll be out in a minute."

They were soon on their way to the office.

Conrad asked Ron, "Have you ever considered selling your Monterey condominium?"

Rod's thinking was slower these days, so responding took a moment.

"Yes, both places are not what you would call handicap friendly. I have to think about the future. I might sell both and get a bigger home this time. Something that allows a wheelchair to get around. You know, Conrad, that time is coming fairly soon."

"You're not there yet, are you?"

"I'm not sure. Things are getting harder for me. You'll have to watch me so I don't do something stupid."

"I can't imagine you doing *anything* stupid."

"I'm serious, Conrad. I almost used the toilet brush as a toothbrush. Okay, I was kidding, but my mind doesn't work now. See, I forgot to call you to let you know that our attorney will be in our meeting this morning."

"That's good, Rod. I think we will need all the help we can get. Did you tell Cindy about this new development in the office building?"

Rod paused, "I may have a problem with Cindy."

Conrad almost lost control of the car, "What?"

"Well, she told me she bumped into this guy, literally. By what she said, he's tall, blond, and good-looking. She didn't know who he was. It happened at a store downtown. Well, Cindy's folks had a big shin-dig dinner at their estate, and guess who showed up? Yep, the tall, blond, and good-looking guy she had bumped into that morning. They walked after dinner, and he asked her out when he left. It wasn't until he left that Cindy remembered about us."

Conrad looked at Rod for a moment. He could see the pain. "Maybe, you're making too big of a deal about it. You know, old family friends."

"Maybe, but I told her to go ahead on a date. What can it hurt? You know Conrad, a woman must be sure before committing a life-long commitment. I guess that should be true for a man also."

"I think you're crazy. You can't let a good woman get away."

"Now, that's great advice. I should handcuff Cindy to a tree or a chair in the Royston home?"

Aaron pulled out his cell phone and called his son, James.

"Hello, James; what are you up to today?"

"Nothing; how are you today. I hear you saw William the other day?"

"I'm fine. I need to apologize to you. Can we meet today?"

"Sure, your office?"

"No, too stuffy here. How about that restaurant we used to go to."

"Okay with me, what time?"

Aaron checked his watch, "Let's make it eleven-thirty."

"See you then, Dad. Thanks for calling. Bye."

Rod had Susan order some donuts for the meeting. She arranged Rod's Conference Table for comfortable four-place seating. She also had a side table for refreshments.

At nine, Rod's attorney and accountant arrived, and Susan told them that Rod and Conrad were in Rod's office.

"Hello, Bill, and Gary, right on time. Have a seat at the Conference Table. I'll be right over."

They all shook hands and sat down.

Bill asked, "How are you feeling, Rod?"

As Rod came around his desk, "I'm okay. Parkinson's is getting harder every day. Let's get started."

Rod laid out his and Conrad's plans for the building. Conrad helped by giving Bill and Gary the facts and figures about the building. For the next two hours, the discussion went back and forth. The attorney, Bill, presented them with what he thought were the good and bad things about ownership of a larger office building. Rod questioned whether the Carson Detective Agency should remain on the bottom floor or move to the second floor.

They did take a break about halfway through the meeting.

After the break, Gary described Rod's financial situation. Conrad had spoken to his accountant and added his comments.

As the discussion wined down. Rod asked, "Okay, gentlemen," as he addressed Bill and Gary, "Give us your bottom line. Bill, go first as our attorney."

"It would be a sound and expensive investment. If you decide to purchase this building, Gary and I should be there when you meet with the Marrone boys."

Gary looked at Rod, "The only real worry I have, Rod, is your health. You know you have the means to purchase with the extensive amount of money you made a couple of years ago with those two large cases. The Bank we went to the other day confirmed that a loan for the remainder of the amount would not be a problem. I would offer at first seven points five, and we can negotiate up to eight million. I feel that should be your top dollar amount."

Rod stood and walked around the room to get the kinks out of his legs and to have time to think.

He then looked at Conrad, who shook his head. Yes, "Let's do it, Conrad. Gary, how much do we put in to lower the loan amount?"

Gary responded, "Rod, you have plenty to put in one point five million, and Conrad, with your five hundred thousand, that would make the loan from five point five to six million. How do you both feel about that amount?"

Rod and Conrad looked at each other again.

Rod said solemnly," Yes, I'll call Jason Marrone for a meeting. How about tomorrow at ten in the morning."

All agreed. After Bill and Gary left, Rod shook hands with Conrad and moved behind his desk to call Jason.

Aaron arrived at the restaurant early. He sat at their favorite booth, where Aaron knew James would easily find him. James arrived on time, and Aaron rose to hug him as he came over. The waitress came over to get their drink order. After she left, James said, "Dad, you did not have to apologize to me earlier. I'm the one who screwed up and kept my mouth shut when I should have told you something was going on."

The waitress came over with their drinks and took their order for food.

After she left, Aaron said, "No, I should apologize to you for not being a dad that would listen, forgive, and love his son. Your mom was the one who had a soft heart. I didn't learn from her. My secretary Ann helped me see the error of my ways with William. She also gave me great advice about you. So here we are, and will you forgive me."

"I'm still the one who needs to handle things better."

Aaron blessed the food when it arrived, then said, "How much did you know about William and our CFO's scam?"

"Really, not much. Enough to know something was not right. I put two and two together, went to William, and asked what was happening. He told me to keep quiet and to keep out of his affairs. He got very angry with me. I don't know why I didn't come to you."

"That's water under a bridge now," Aaron responded, "What did you learn from that episode?"

"Dad, I took a long vacation to Hawaii to clear my head. I was there for two months. During that time, I grew up a lot. I took stock for the first time, and what I saw was not good. I had to change. I had to forgive myself."

Aaron took his time responding to what James said, "I kind of know what you're saying. See, it's hard to see and admit my mistakes when everything is going great. I failed you in many ways. I failed my executives in many ways. I failed to see what Harold Grayson, our CFO, was doing. I now have a leadership model that will help each person and hopefully prevent anything like the former Chief Financial Officer did."

"That's great, Dad. I guess we both learned something."

Aaron continued, "I've got a plan to help both of us. Sterling, Inc. has a new CFO and a new CEO. They're wonderful people, and I want you to return to be the CEO's assistant. His name is Dennis Gilbert. You have so much knowledge about our company that you would be an asset to him. We could see about getting your old job title back."

James was moved by his dad's comments, "Are you sure? Is this really what you want me to do?"

"Yes, it is. I see a change in you. This makes me very encouraged. Why don't you come back to work."

"Okay, make it Monday. I've got some things to do. See you then. You can count on me."

CHAPTER EIGHTEEN

The historical meeting for the possible purchase of the building was all set for ten that morning. Susan had gone out of her way to make everything just right. Plenty of refreshments on a couple of side tables on both sides of the large Conference Room. Donuts, cheese, crackers, and a veggie dish with Ranch Dressing all looked delicious. Susan had enough soft drinks, lemonade, and water for a small army. She wiped the furniture to ensure the whole room looked right and stood back to see if it was enough.

Rod found Susan, "This place looks fantastic. Did you spend all night here?"

"No, I know how important this meeting is for our company's future. The other girls here pitched in, and we worked hard to make everything as perfect as possible."

Rod nodded yes, "I can tell you spent a lot of time setting it up. Thank you. Don't be nervous. My mom used to say, 'It all comes out in the wash.' I don't have any idea what that means either."

They both laughed. Susan turned to find Jordan to ask another question. Evidently, the ladies wanted to have the offices looking neat and professional.

Rod and Conrad greeted Jason and Ryan Marrone as they entered the office of the Carson Detective Agency. The Marrones brought their accountant and attorney. Susan was happy that she had thought they might also be coming. Susan will be attending to record the meeting.

When all the attendees fixed a plate of goodies and drinks, they sat down.

Rod started the meeting, "Let's make sure everyone knows who is here. So if everyone introduces themselves, then we can be more informal."

After the introductions, Rod began, "I'm sure all of us are ready and excited to get this meeting going. Just some background, Jason and Ryan came to us some time back. They asked if we, the Carson Detective Agency, were considering purchasing this building. We said we had been talking about it but needed some time to crunch numbers and talk about it. That's why we are having this meeting to discuss those possibilities."

Rod sipped his coffee, "After our meeting yesterday with the accountant and Lawyer, Gary, and Bill, we called you, Jason, to come here and meet. Does that cover it, Jason?"

"Yes, it does, Rod."

"Okay, let's get started. What is the asking price?"

"I like you get right down to the point. The checking we have done runs anywhere between seven and nine million. What would you offer?"

Rod cleared his throat, "These numbers get me choked up. We can start the negotiations at seven point five million."

Jason looked at his brother, "Ryan and I have been doing some serious talking. First of all, we had no idea it would be so much. But after consultation with our attorney and accountant and remembering the struggle Dad had to keep his detective company going, we have decided to double that amount."

A hush came over the room; even Jason and Ryan's accountant and lawyer looked at Jason with their mouths open.

Jason gave a long pause. Then started laughing, "Just kidding!"

Rod had to catch his breath, "You definitely had me there, Jason. Before you continue, I need another drink."

Everyone laughed, but Jason soon continued, "Sorry about that."

Conrad responded, "No, you're not."

They all laughed again.

"Seriously, Rod, you revived Dad from a sad man to a new man with much to look forward to. Ryan and I are in good shape financially, so here's our proposal."

Rod and Conrad leaned forward.

"Six point two million."

The air in the room seemed to disappear for Rod, Conrad, Bill, and Gary. They looked at each other. No one could speak.

Rod's attorney, Bill, said, "Are you sure. You know the market says eight or eight and a half million is a fair price."

Ryan stood and said with tears in his eyes, "You people don't understand how much our dad meant to us. He's gone way too early. Like Jason said, this is what we want. Rod and Conrad, this is like a thank-you for what you did for Dad. I and neither will Jason, look back at our decision with any regrets. Jason is well settled in his business, and now that he will be moving into Dad's paid-for home, he will do even better. Frankly, I'm making more money now. I don't know what to do with it all."

His accountant said, "Invest it, son, invest it."

Jason then also stood, "Are we in agreement, Rod?"

"Yes, we agree. I'm sure our attorneys will communicate with each other about the paperwork that we need to sign. Thank you, Jason and Ryan. That's so generous."

Rod and Conrad stood around the table to shake hands with Ryan and Jason and hug them.

After the meeting, Conrad entered Rod's office with a bottle of wine and three glasses. Susan joined them in a toast.

Marcus and Javier were almost back down to the Castle Domes area when they came across two Park Rangers.

Javier asked them, "What's it like on the other side of Castle Domes?"

One of the Rangers thought briefly, "I think I'm the only one that's been back in that area. It's kind of desolate and dangerous. Something is going on over there. I've seen a bunch of vultures circling in that area."

Marcus responded, "I thought that was just in the movies?"

The Ranger, named Howard, replied, "Actually, birds, especially scavengers which have an enhanced sense of smell, will fly in circles when they find a carcass or a dead animal. They can use thermals to hover. They wait for other animals, like bears or wolves, to complete the meal before they descend to feast on the remains."

Marcus looked at Javier, "Are you thinking what I'm thinking about? Could it be who we're looking for?"

Javier asked Howard, "Could one of you or both come

with us to the other side and check it out?"

Howard, who said he had been to the other side of Castle Domes, replied, "I'll have to get permission from the higher-ups to go with you. I'd like to accompany you there."

Howard called his boss and received an okay to go with Marcus and Javier.

Howard suggested they spend the night on Castle Domes Meadow before taking off in the morning.

The meadow was exciting, with tall grass, boulders, and other minor rocks. Woods Creek ran the valley length, and the cold water was soothing. Bears came down this low in the mountains occasionally. There also were rattlesnakes that liked to feel the sun on the trails.

The Park Ranger, Howard, Marcus, and Javier decided to have a big dinner because they wanted an early start in the morning. They would only do some snacking when they started the hike. The Park Ranger prepared the dinner because he had more supplies for food.

"It will feel great to get some good sleep tonight," Javier told Marcus.

Marcus replied, "That sounds awesome to me also. Early to bed, early to rise."

"Whatever."

Cory called Cindy and asked if today would be okay for a date.

Cindy hesitated, "Yes, today is fine. Lunch or dinner? Casual or formal?

"Wow, okay, lunch and casual. How about twelve-thirty?

"Sounds good, see you then," Cindy sat back and

thought, *What did I get myself into?*

Just before the arranged time, Cory entered the Roystons drive in a brand new Cadillac Escalade-V with the color Cadillac calls Radiant Red.

Cindy could not believe what she saw because she had chosen an almost identical color pantsuit. This can either go good or bad. He escorted her to the car and opened the door.

Cindy thought, *One good point: I'm looking for ten good points.*

Cory took her to a charming casual/dressy restaurant in Napa.

So far, so good. Two points.

Dinner went perfectly. Cory asked, "Tell me about yourself. I would like to know more about you."

"I went to the California College of the Arts. Majored in Piano. I have a music store in Napa to teach students piano. I have twelve keyboards. Each student turns off the sound and listens through headphones. I can listen to each one on my headphones to see how they're doing."

Cory replied, "What's the name of your store?"

"Napa Notes."

"That's very clever. So, you have free time today?"

"No, I have different sessions during the year. Right now, I have five sessions a year. I also have another teacher. We alternate sessions, so we both have plenty of time off. Tell me more about yourself."

"I'm a graduate of UCLA School of Law. My dad, Arlo, as you know, is a big wheel in the U.S. Government. We are very close and enjoy every time we get together. We haven't had much time to have some fun since I left Law School. Did I mention that I am single and dating no one presently?"

Cindy thought, *TMI, two points down.*

"Do you have your own firm, or are you in a group?"

"At the time, I'm a Junior Associate Lawyer in a firm. When I get enough experience, I would like to have my own firm."

He's too busy now for a dating life. He's under average by one point.

"That's wonderful, Cory. I bet you don't have much time for social activities."

"I do my best to get out there. I like golf, and it gets me involved with clients and fellow lawyers."

The conversation went in different directions. This gave Cindy time to think about her next move with Cory. Cory took her for a drive in the hills about Napa. Cindy had seen all this before but wanted to be gracious, so she enjoyed the ride and conversation.

Cory eventually took Cindy home. When he escorted her to the door, she knew what he might ask next, and she was ready.

When he asked her, Cindy said, "Cory, I am seeing someone else on dates."

Cory responded, "That's okay. Let's try one more date and see what happens. I'll call you in a few days if that's okay."

"Okay, thanks for the dinner and lovely drive. Talk to you soon."

Cindy turned and went inside.

The following morning, Marcus and Javier woke up to the smell of coffee and some breakfast. Absolutely nothing smells better in the mountains when you're waking up. They got up quickly and went to the campfire for coffee and some scrambled eggs. Even if the eggs were fake, they tasted outstanding.

Javier told Howard, "Hey, I thought we were only going to have some snacks as we started the hike."

Howard scooped up some more eggs, "I got up real early, so I decided to splurge and have a decent breakfast."

Marcus was up and packing his gear, "Sounds good to me. Thanks a lot, Howard."

A woman approached them on the meadow when they had finished their meal and packed their gear.

The senior Park Ranger stopped her to ask some questions. "What is your name, and are you alone?"

"My name is Becky Savage, and my partner and I became separated over a week ago. I got lost, and some hikers found me two days ago in the Fin Dome and Mount Cotter area. I camped last night at the John Muir Trail cutoff."

The Park Ranger asked, "Do you have some identification on you?"

Becky took her backpack off, searched in one of the pockets for her small purse, and handed him her driver's license and hiking permit.

After examining the documents, he said, "I'm going to have to escort you to the trailhead and then to the Fresno Police Department."

She responded, "Why? I haven't done anything."

"A detective with the Fresno PD has some questions he needs to ask you about your missing partner."

"You mean he hasn't shown up yet?"

"Let me get my gear, and we can head for the trailhead. Is your car there?"

"No, he drove his car. My car is at my home."

The Park Ranger said, "Okay, Let's go."

In San Jose, Rod and Conrad met with the remainder of the staff at their office.

Conrad told them, "I know we're shorthanded until our Fresno and Kings Canyon National Park detectives return. You have been steady workers and even working overtime to keep us in business. I commend our detectives, Jerry and Eva, for your round-the-clock work to keep up with business. Our newest detective in Monterey, Larry Groves, has also kept himself busy in our southern California office. I will be looking for another detective there in that area."

Rod spoke, "I appreciate your continued service. This agency has and is getting nationwide exposure."

Conrad continued, "Rod and I met with the Marrone boys yesterday. We can now tell you that the Carson Detective Agency has purchased this building. The tenants we have now will stay with us. We will be hiring a full-time manager for the Carson Building. This purchase should not affect our business. However, we are considering possibly moving to the second floor to get a higher rent or lease for these offices. Remember, we're just thinking about this, so don't pack your bags....Yet."

After the group settled down, Rod said, "Are there any questions? If not, let's get back to work."

Conrad followed Rod to Rod's office, "Boss, let's take another walk upstairs and see if moving there is even possible."

Cindy received another call from Cory asking her for

another date.

Cindy replied, "Okay, Cory. When do you want to go out?"

"Tonight would be good for me."

"Not tonight; my family has plans for tonight. How about tomorrow night?"

Cory responded, "Sounds good. I'll pick you up at five-thirty."

"Okay. Bye."

After Cindy got off the phone, she went to her room to think. She loved to sit by her window to read or to think. *Why was I dating a man other than Rod? It's about time to get my feelings under control,* she thought. *What do I really know about Cory? Not much.*

For the next hour, she decided to write down her feelings. Why did Rod mean so much to her? Does Rod's Parkinson's affect their relationship? Cory is not stacking up to what she wants in a man.

After she read and re-read her notes, she came to an answer.

It was late afternoon when Becky Savage was transported to Fresno by Fresno police officers. After arriving at the Fresno Police Department, she was escorted to the Homicide Division. Lead homicide detective Juan Garcia had her placed in an interview room.

Juan asked Becky, "Tell me about your Kings Canyon National Park hike. Who were you with? What caused the separation? Where did you last see the person you were with? Where did you spend your nights?"

Becky took the water they had offered her, "I was with

Al Fletcher. I suppose you know that by now. We are co-owners of Fresno Fitness Club. We wanted to only be away for a few days in the park. We were headed for the Rae Lakes region, and Arrowhead Lake is where we got separated. I had no idea where he went. I walked around the lake, and when I got back, he was gone. I stayed there that night. I hollered for him in the morning, but he never returned."

Juan took his time and leaned back, "Tell me about your business and how it was doing? Did he have any enemies?"

She talked about their business and Al's friends and adversaries for the next hour. Near the end, Becky asked if they had found Al. Juan did not know if he should tell her. He would wait a while to check on some things. He did not release her when she asked if she could leave because Juan wanted more answers.

Becky did not like that.

CHAPTER NINETEEN

When Marcus, Javier and Howard, the Park Ranger left the Castle Domes Meadow, it was a gorgeous day. The Domes is a beautiful scenic location. But soon, they came upon aspens and junipers growing between the majestic tall craggy cliff-side that encircled the area. Howard advised Javier and Marcus that rattlesnakes were sighted around this region, so be careful. He said to watch out where you put your hands and feet. The Ranger took the lead in case he saw any, and besides, he knew the best way around the Domes.

They reached the other side of Castle Domes in mid-afternoon. They were beside a lovely flowing brook when Howard said they would stay there for the night and proceed in the morning. Howard explained that they still had a ways to go, so they needed a good night's sleep.

Marcus told Javier, "That was quite a climb coming up here. I can see why someone could get hurt because the trail, at times, is so rocky and single-file walking. Did you notice those vultures flying around?"

"Yes, I did. As far as we know, Rogers Brooks is the only one missing. I'm anxious to see what kind of an animal is dead. If it's an animal."

Early the following day, after breakfast and packing. They headed out to search the area where the birds were flying around. Howard told them they were hours away because they would encounter some bad spots for hiking. He told them to be careful.

They were at a spot where they could see for quite a distance ahead.

Howard pulled out his binoculars to look at the spot where the birds were flying. He saw a bear and a few coyotes but couldn't see what drew them there to that location. They had over a mile of up-and-down hiking in some rugged terrain before they arrived at the scene.

When the group was about a hundred yards away from the scene, Howard held up his hand for them to stop.

Howard said, "I see the bear now, and something is on the ground that he is eating. Probably a deer. I'll see if I can scare off the bear and get close enough to what the carcass is. If the bear is hungry, it might be harder to chase away. Follow me about halfway and stop. If he charges, you are free to shoot."

Howard was carrying an AK-47. That rifle takes a 7.62mm cartridge that would bring down almost anything. But a charging angry bear? Maybe not the first shot.

Javier was carrying a heavier handgun than Marcus, so he took it out and ensured it was loaded and ready to go. The trail was for one person only, so as they approached mid-point, the bear raised his snout, testing the smells. His head came around to where they were closing.

Howard started hollering and throwing rocks to try to scare off the bear. It was not working.

Howard took his rifle and placed a larger clip into the AK-47. Howard took some more steps and stopped. He turned to Javier, "I don't want to, but I may have to kill this bear. I've seen this one, but he's in a bad mood. If he charges, start shooting when I start shooting, Okay?"

"I'm right behind you but in a safe place to shoot if necessary. I don't want to shoot also. Such a beautiful animal."

Howard responded, "We may not want to, but he may be a killer, so here goes."

They were within one hundred feet when the enormous male black bear rose on his hind feet and roared. The hair on all three men spiked at the sound.

They took a few more steps.

The bear dropped and charged.

In the Fresno PD interview room, Becky wanted to talk to Juan. Juan came in a minute later.

"Yes, what do you want?"

"I want a lawyer."

"Okay, do you have one, or should we get one for you?"

"We have a business lawyer, but you should get me one."

Juan replied, "Okay, but it may take some time before we can locate one."

"Can I go until one comes in?"

"No, you may sit down. Do you need anything to eat or drink?"

After Juan received what she wanted to eat and drink, he told her to stay there. He said he would order it right away. Becky could have been a happier camper. She didn't have her purse or phone.

Juan discussed the case with the other detectives. They all concluded that Becky should remain in custody for at least forty-eight hours. She might have more information that would be crucial to the investigation. But their hands were tied because she asked for a lawyer. Juan knew a couple of criminal lawyers, so he made some phone calls. The first one he called was available and said he would be right in.

When the lawyer arrived, he asked Juan how long they would hold her. Juan told him he would like to see if she had more information about Al's location and possible killer or killers. He also informed the lawyer that he had not told her Al was dead, but Juan wanted to see her reaction. The lawyer agreed not to tell her until Juan entered the interview room.

Juan gave the lawyer enough time to introduce himself to Becky and give her some instructions before Juan entered the room.

Juan explained that he needed as much information as Becky had to help find who murdered Al. Becky started to cry and took some tissues. Juan asked again if she had thought of anything new that might help. Becky said she didn't know of any other information that would help. Juan carefully watched Becky. Juan went back to his office and wrote a lot of notes. Something had to click soon, or this might be a cold case. He didn't want that at all. Juan liked to finish his cases as quickly as possible.

Juan called the Medical Examiner again, "Anything come back from your tests on the Al Fletcher case?"

"Not yet, Juan. I am interested in the evidence I took from underneath his fingernails."

"Do you think I should try to get blood samples from his partner?"

"That might be a good idea."

Juan went back into the interview room. He asked if

it would be okay for them to take a blood sample from Becky. Becky looked at the lawyer. He wondered if she was a suspect. Juan answered negatively, but she would be eliminated from the suspect list once the tests returned.

The lawyer said it was necessary, and he didn't want them to get a court order because that would look like she had something to hide,

Juan ordered the tests to be made on Becky. Juan was happy that the Lawyer spoke as he did to her.

Becky was still not happy.

A bunch of shots rang out and echoed through the mountains. The Park Ranger, Howard, must have shot six times before the enormous black bundle of fur fell not over twenty feet away. Javier also fired at least three times but was still determined, in his state of mind, if he hit anything. He looked around at Marcus. Javier thought Marcus was on his way to becoming sick.

"You look terrible, Marcus; you need to sit down.?"

Marcus was visually shaken, "I have never seen anything like it. I have shot people before but nothing like this. Wow."

The Park Ranger started forward slowly. Javier was right behind Howard.

Howard raised his hand, "You may not want to see this."

Javier came forward anyway.

What they saw made their skin crawl. What they saw was the remains of a human. The body was so chewed up that even its face was obliterated. It could only be described as a mangled mess. Howard had to turn away and heave. Javier was almost at that point, but he had seen enough crime scenes to know how to set up a crime scene. He thought at first it was a bear attack, but his instincts told him to look at it in a different light.

"Howard, Marcus, and I will treat this as a crime scene until we know something else."

Howard responded, "I've seen a couple of people over the years that had bear attacks, but nothing like this. Those people survived their wounds. I'm calling in for the Ranger in Charge of this Park and ask him to bring in a helicopter with a body bag."

Marcus and Javier scoured the area. After a few minutes, Javier said, "Marcus, I think this person did not die here. I believe he or she was dragged here. Let's see if we can follow the tracks.

Drag marks and bear tracks showed that the body was moved to where they found it.

The signs led them to the edge of a cliff. They found some rocks in the immediate area that seemed to have fallen recently. Marcus found the spot where he thought the person had fallen. A pool of dried blood revealed to them the possibility of a compound fracture.

Javier took a very close look at the scene. He took out his phone and started to take a lot of pictures. Then he yelled to Marcus, "Come look at this."

In the dirt at the base of the cliff, Javier found something that sent shockwaves through him. The person had written, *Love you, mom and d-----*.

Of course, Cory was right on time for their date. Cindy still had some doubts but decided to wait and enjoy herself.

Cory said, "Cindy, you seem a little different tonight. Is

something wrong?"

"No, I'm fine." She lied, "Let's enjoy the evening."

Cory kept checking his phone. Cindy thought he was checking the directions to the restaurant.

During the meal, the conversation was cordial, but he kept checking his phone about every five minutes.

One point off, every time he checked his phone, Cindy thought. *That's the final nail in the coffin.*

After dinner, Cindy said, "Would you mind taking me home. I have a splitting headache. I've had one all day."

"Okay, let's get you home," he said as he paid for the meal.

When they got to Cindy's home, She turned to Cory and said, "Cory, It's more than a headache. I need to be honest with you. I have been dating a dear friend for a long time now. After you and I spoke on the phone today, I went to my bedroom to my favorite window, where I did my reading and thinking. I had to, first of all, be honest with myself. You know, facing some facts, knowing who I am and what I want in life."

Cindy said, "Cory, you are a good-looking gentleman with a lot going for you. Thank you for the fun dates, but I know now who I want to spend my life with and have a family with, Rod, my close friend. Sorry."

Cory looked down at Cindy and put his hand on her shoulder, "I think I knew what you were going to say before you said it. Cindy, you're a wonderful, gorgeous woman. But we all must come to that proverbial fork in the road to make a wise decision. Thank you for being honest. May I walk you to the door?"

"Of course, you may."

They ambled to the door. At the entrance, Cory turned and kissed Cindy on the cheek, "Maybe we'll bump into each other some other time. Goodnight."

They both turned as Cindy entered her home, and Cory slowly returned to his car. Before getting in, he stood there for a moment. Turning with a respectful smile, he got back into his car and drove out of the driveway.

He picked up Sue at his home in Camarillo. Aaron had decided to stay in an apartment in LA since He and Sue were engaged. Both of them knew that even at their age, the temptation was a factor in that decision not to stay in the same house until their wedding night.

"You look great tonight, Sue. Well, I must say that you always look great. But especially tonight. Maybe it's because I am anxious about our wedding in a few weeks. I've got an idea. Could we elope tonight?"

Sue couldn't tell if he was serious until a cunning smile crossed his face.

"Oh, you're in a lot of trouble. I almost said, Yes."

They both hugged and snickered at that thought.

Aaron and Sue were getting to know each other. Their love for each other seemed to grow every minute they were together. All the pieces of the wedding puzzle fell into place. Sue was not as nervous as she was.

Aaron and Sue were in love.

CHAPTER TWENTY

Preparation for the wedding was at full speed. Camarillo Community Church was booked for the wedding ceremony. The pastor had been meeting with Aaron and Sue for some weeks. Flowers were ordered, and the wedding party had been notified much earlier. The reception was planned, and Aaron's private secretary, Ann, was a bundle of nerves getting everything ready because she was in charge. Ann picked the perfect Country Club for the occasion.

Ann had helped Sue previously pick out the perfect wedding dress in a fancy Beverly Hills Wedding Shoppe.

All the planning was done, and nothing should go wrong?!?!

Sue had long picked Ann as her Bridesmaid, and Aaron asked his oldest son James to be his Best man. Aaron also wanted Rod to stand beside the best man, but Rod declined. With Parkinson's, Rod told Aaron he couldn't stand that long. He sure would be at the wedding because Sue had asked Rod to walk with her down the aisle to give her away. Conrad would be one of the men standing with Aaron's son James.

Aaron and his driver stopped to pick up Sue in their new stretch limousine. The shiny black limo came around the circular driveway in Spanish Hills, an exclusive section of Camarillo.

The driver hurried around the limo to help Sue to her seat. Aaron had decided to take her to a fancy, pricy restaurant in Ventura, California. The Aloha Steakhouse was known for its Seafood and Prime Rib dinners. Unknown to Sue, Aaron had called and made a reservation for the best window view of the ocean.

As soon as Sue was seated, she said, "Aaron, you called ahead to get this seat and view. Didn't you?"

"Yes, I did, but nothing is too special for my gal. Enjoy the evening. Take your time and get whatever you want."

Aaron explained the menu, and the dishes were outstanding, "If you like Prime Rib, they have *the* best."

After the drinks and order were taken, Aaron pointed out the window. The most gorgeous sunset was about to take place. A waiter came by and asked if he could take a picture with Aaron's phone to capture the ambiance of the moment.

They took their time with the meal and dessert. Aaron selected a particular brand of wine that he knew they both liked.

A perfect ending to an unforgettable night of dining.

They were finishing up when Sue's phone rang.

She answered because it was her mother, "Oh, no." Sue said, "I'll be up as soon as I can. What hospital?"

Aaron was very concerned, "One of the children?"

"Yes, Joshua had a bad fall, and they are taking him by ambulance to Community Hospital in Monterey."

Aaron responded, "I'm sure he'll be okay. Let me call my driver and alert him that we have to go to Monterey."

"Oh, I hate to ruin your evening. I'm sorry."

"What are you talking about? Sue, Josh, and Julianne will soon be my kids also."

"You're right; sorry again."

They were soon on their way for a four-and-a-half-hour trip. Aaron's driver advised him that they would have to stop in San Luis Obispo for gas.

A little over four hours later, they arrived at the Community Hospital. Aaron and Sue went to the information desk to find her son's location.

It was a wild night in the Emergency Room. After a nurse talked to them, they were escorted to her son's room.

They walked in and saw this big cast on his left arm.

When Joshua saw them, he said, "Mom and Dad, will you sign my cast?"

Relief flowed from Sue as she sat down beside Joshua. She

asked Aaron, "Did you hear what he called you?"

"Yes, I did," Aaron said with an enormous grin.

Sue's mother came and was so happy that Aaron and Sue were there. Sue saw the deep worry and concern in her mom.

"Mom, what happened?"

"You know, boys. That big tree out back of our house, well, he had to see how high he could get. Thank God I didn't see it, but he told me what had happened when he came in. His arm didn't look right, so I called 9-1-1. They came and said he needed to go to the hospital."

Aaron thought; so *much for a quiet, excellent dinner date.*

Juan Garcia had difficulty reviewing the facts and evidence from Al Fletcher's murder. Some things were not adding up. Juan sure wished the test results would come in. It's never like TV shows. In reality, it takes a long time. Sometimes months.

The Chief of Police in Fresno came by Juan's office.

"How's the Fletcher case coming along?" The Chief asked.

"Chief, some things are not adding up. Timelines don't line up with the facts. I'm sure Derik Thomson did it, but I can't tie him to it yet. Can't wait for the Medical Examiner's test to come back in. That might give me a clear answer. I must let him walk if I can't produce clear evidence. I don't even have a motive yet. At least not a good one."

The Chief responded, "Keep at it, Juan. You're a great detective. The puzzle pieces will come into place at the right time."

"Oh, Chief," Juan said before the Chief got away, "Did you hear they found some mangled remains up at Kings Canyon National Park? They had to kill a bear at the scene. I just received a call from the Head of Park Rangers for Kings Canyon. They're bringing a helicopter to remove and bring the remains here to the Fresno morgue."

"Any ID on the body?" The Chief asked.

"No, and the body is in such bad shape, they couldn't tell if it's a man or woman or teenager."

The Chief added, "The Medical Examiner will come up with

the ID.

The Chief of Police smiled and went back to his domain. Juan started going through his notes again, starting at the top. Juan felt he had missed something, so he slowly, carefully, and thoughtfully reviewed his notes and evidence again. It's there someplace; the answer is never easy.

"Hi there. You look very busy. You want me to come back later?" Jada said at Juan's office door.

"No. In fact, you might be able to see something I missed. Pull that chair beside me, and I'll start at the top again and give you the sheet I'm reading after I finish it. Let's go very slowly and think through each item."

Jada adjusted the nearest chair beside him at his desk. The process was slow, but she understood that good police work is not fast because it's easy to miss something.

Jada asked Juan, "Let me get some of that wonderful police break room coffee while you study that paper."

"Okay, remember, I like it black. No offense," Juan said as he smiled at her.

Jada chuckled as she left the room.

When she returned with the coffee, she noticed that Juan was still on the first page, "You are taking your time."

"Things are not adding up, so I don't want to miss anything. Let's see what you come up with."

The rest of the morning, two people worked side by side, quietly, until Jada said, "Look at the ligature marks again. My mind tells me that the wounds on his neck are not true to something people would use to strangle someone. I mean, they're not wire type or rope size. Look here near his Adam's apple. What does that look like to you?"

"Let's see."

"That's an unusual mark. What do you make of it.?"

Jada leaned over and pointed, "At first, I thought it was a knot of some sort."

Juan looked at her, "You know, you may be right. What would be tied together to make a strangling weapon?"

"Shoelaces."

"Joe Brooks is having a conniption fit," Conrad told Rod.

"What in the world is a conniption fit?"

"You never heard of a conniption fit? You mean the all-knowing, all-seeing magnificent Rod Carson doesn't know what a conniption fit is?"

"Okay, smarty, what is it?"

"Well, are you ready?"

"YES. I'm ready." Rod shouted.

"A conniption fit is….a sudden outburst of excitement or anger."

"Conrad, did you memorize that out of the dictionary?"

"Ah, Yes."

"Conrad, tell me about Joe. What's going on?"

"He called me early this morning, I mean early."

"Okay, Conrad, is this one of those Knock-Knock Jokes?"

"No, I'm sorry. Joe was like, feeling like he couldn't take it anymore. He doesn't know what to do with his wife, Dawn. She is driving him crazy. If we don't know about his son soon, he is leaving for Kings Canyon National Park to look for Roger."

Rod responded, "I'll give him a call. There's not much I can tell him."

"Rod, I received a call from the Head of the Park Rangers. You may not want to hear this."

"Parkinson's doesn't affect my hearing or reasoning so far."

"Javier, Marcus, and a Park Ranger found a badly mangled body yesterday. They can't even tell the sex or age of the person. They flew the remains to the Medical Examiner in Fresno. It's going to take some time to ID the person. They also said they had to kill a huge black bear at the scene. When Marcus and Javier get off the mountains and return to Fresno, they will call me and give me the details."

Rod looked worried, "That had to be awful seeing that body. Keep me informed. I won't tell Joe Brooks about this new development. That might send him over the edge. We don't know any other missing persons up there, do we?"

"No, the Head Park Ranger said they had not been in contact

with all the hikers around that area. It could be anyone."

Conrad went back to his office, and Rod called Joe.

"Joe? This is Rod; what can I do to help?"

"Nothing Rod, It's been too long. Any news yet? Dawn is almost having a nervous breakdown. I'm not in better shape, myself."

"Nothing new, Joe. All we can do is continue to pray."

Joe responded, "That's all we've been doing. It seems our prayers don't go beyond the ceiling."

"Joe, I know you need answers. I don't have them yet. I don't know why, but many people are working hard to find Roger."

Joe paused, "I know, Rod. At this point, between you and me, if we could hear, even if you've found his body."

"Joe, I don't think it will be much longer."

When they finished the call, Rod sat back. Lord, *Please answer Joe's prayer. One way or another.*

CHAPTER TWENTY-ONE

Two days later there was a lot of activity at the Fresno Police Department. The Fresno County Medical Examiner contacted Fresno PD's head detective, Juan Garcia.

Juan gave Jada a call.

"Jada, can you come to my office? I have some news for you."

Fifteen minutes later, Jada entered Juan's office.

"Have a seat, Jada. The mangled body is Roger Brooks. The Medical Examiner was able to find a usable fingerprint to identify him. They knew the importance of that case, so they did a rush job. The M.E. declared Roger not to be a homicide. With all the facts, it seems he died soon after he fell off a cliff. I don't know if I told you, but he wrote in the dirt before the bear dragged him to another area."

"Wow, that's going to wallop his family. What did he write in the dirt?"

"He wrote, *love you, mom,* and the letter *d*. Marcus and Javier believe either he died then or the bear dragged him away. They think he was already dead or near death when the bear took him."

Jada sat back in her chair, "Can I use the conference room to make a private call to my boss?"

"Close the door, and you will not be disturbed."

She left Juan's office and entered the conference room.

"Conrad, are you alone?"

"Yes, what's up?"

"The Fresno County Medical Examiner identified that badly messed up body as Roger Brooks. She could find an intact finger to fingerprint for the ID."

"No, that's going to strike them tough. Thanks for letting me know. I'll go let Rod know now. I'll also see if he's in shape to make the call. Whoever makes that call, it will be hard."

Conrad slowly went to Rod's office and knocked on the door.

"Come in," Rod said.

"Rod, how are you feeling?"

"I'm okay; what's on your mind."

"Boss, I just received a call from Jada. She was just told that the body they brought from Kings Canyon National Park had been identified. It's definitely Roger Brooks."

"Oh, No. The news will be devastating to Joe and his family."

"Do you want me to make the call?"

"No, Conrad. That's my job. Good or bad news must come from the top person. So far, that's me. Thank you for asking. It will not be easy. I'll try to do it in person, but if I knew Joe, he would want it immediately."

"Okay, boss. I'll shut your door on the way out and tell Susan not to disturb you until you come out."

After Conrad left, Rod put his head back on his executive chair, and the thought came to him. *Lord, help me deliver this news to Joe in a compassionate and empathetic manner.*

"Joe, this is Rod. Got It. Call me back right away."

"Okay, I will drive to a park around the corner. It won't be long."

After about five minutes, Rod's phone rang again, "Hello."

"Rod, what's the news. Don't beat around the bush, Okay?"

"Okay, Joe. It's not good. They found a body a few days ago. The Fresno Medical Examiner today identified the body to be Roger. I'm so sorry."

Rod could hear sobs from Joe, and he decided to be quiet and wait.

Eventually, the cries subsided, and Rod said again, "I'm sorry."

"Rod, how did it happen?"

"Our detectives, Javier and Marcus, and a Park Ranger found the body from what I have learned. It appears he fell off a cliff. It appears he died from the fall or very soon after. That's all that I know at this moment. Do you want me to come over?"

"No, Rod. I will sit here momentarily, figuring out how to tell my wife and daughter, Angel."

"May I suggest that you contact your pastor first? He will want to be with you when you tell them. Don't try to do this alone. After you tell them, Conrad and I would like to come over. Just let me know when you're ready for us."

"Okay, Rod, thank you for your kindness. I'll talk to you soon. Bye."

Rod felt the load off his back, but it still was not easy. Rod came out of his room, and Susan came to offer condolences.

"Thanks, Susan. That was one of the hardest things I

have ever had to do. Joe and his whole family will be hurting."

Rod received a call from the Neurologist informing him that Rod needed to go back to the hospital, where some tests were done about his Parkinson's.

Rod walked to Conrad's office.

"Conrad, I hope you're not too busy. The Neurologist called and told me I needed to return to that hospital in Oakland to get a procedure done. Of course, these doctors talk to a person in such a way that you would have to have an interpreter to decipher what he said. Anyway, I got the part that I needed to get there, and I may have to stay there a day or two."

Conrad put his pen down, "I was just trying to write some notes before I forget what Marcus told me about finding Roger's body. We'll have to go to your apartment to get some personal stuff. I'm ready if you are."

After they left Rod's apartment to go to the Oakland hospital, Rod decided he had better call Cindy.

"Hi Cindy, how are you today?"

"I'm fine. Just busy. I'm at my piano studio with a couple of students. What's going on?"

"Nothing much; Conrad is driving me to the hospital in Oakland."

"What?"

"Let me finish. The Neurologist called and said he wanted me to have another procedure. Something about one of the tests they did some weeks ago. He said many other things, but I have no idea what it was about. You know how doctors talk."

Cindy responded, "I can call the parents of my students

to come and pick them up, and I'll be on the way."

"No, that's okay. I'll ask Conrad to call you if he thinks it's necessary."

"Well, okay. Whatever you think. Love you. Bye."

Rod turned to Conrad, "Maybe I shouldn't have called her. Now she's worried."

"Is the Neurologist going to meet us there?"

"Yeah, he said to call him when we get there. He said to go to Admittance to check for a room. He said that he had already called the hospital, and they should have a room ready."

After an hour's drive, they approached the hospital.

As they headed to Rod's hospital room, he told Conrad, "The Neurologist must be a big man around here. Did you see how they hurried to get me to that room?"

Rod didn't have to call the doctor because the Admittance called him when Rod came in. It wasn't long before the Neurologist arrived. He wanted to know if talking with Conrad sitting there was okay.

"Sure, He's my number one man at Carson Detective Agency."

The doctor explained again what Rod didn't hear before. Rod finally understood that some liquid in his head needed to come out. The doctor said Rod needed a shunt to drain the liquid out.

After the doctor left, Rod said, "Conrad, he might have said that on the phone, but it seemed much clearer this time."

"Doctors are like that," Conrad said.

"Do you know what a 'shunt' is?"

Conrad reached for his phone, "Let me google it."

Conrad wrote the word SHUNT and waited.

Soon Conrad read from his phone.

"In medicine, *a passage allows blood or other fluid to move from one part of the body to another.*"

Conrad stopped to take a breath.

Rod said, "That's gross."

"Wait till you hear this part; for *example, a surgeon may implant a tube to drain cerebrospinal fluid from the brain to the abdomen.* You got all that?"

"What's *cebrospindle*?"

Conrad read about cerebrospinal, "*It relates to the brain and spine*. It's just a medical term."

Rod thought for a few seconds, "Sounds serious? No wonder they wanted me to come in."

Two nurses told Conrad he had to leave because they would prep Rod for surgery.

"Call Cindy while you're in the waiting room. Don't scare her."

Conrad waved and left the room.

Fresno, California, is known for its hot summers. This day was no different when Juan Garcia gave Jada Davis a call.

"Are you up to a fancy dinner tonight?"

"Sure. I don't have to dress up too much, do I?"

"No, a summer dinner dress or slacks would be fine."

"Okay, maybe around six?" Jada said."

"See you then, bye."

Juan took her to the charming Parma restaurant. The best Italian food in Fresno. She was dressed gorgeously in a light print dress. She brought along a throw sweater because most restaurants turn the temperature down. Juan had arranged for a more secluded table for two away from the bar's noise.

As they were seated, Jada said to Juan, "This is fabulous. You must pull some weight around here."

"I happen to know the manager. I did a favor for her kid that got in some trouble."

The meal was outstanding. The conversation is even better. No shop talks. They found out more about each other. Even some of the wrong things. Jada began to think she was the worst of them both. Juan knew some of her background. It didn't really surprise him when Jada commented about some of her past. Juan had some confessions to make. It made Jada laugh because she thought he never got in trouble. They had a magnificent evening.

The waitress brought the dessert, and Jada noticed a small envelope on the side of the plate.

"What's this?" she said.

Juan said, smiling, "Open it."

Jada gave him a long look, "What's going on. I didn't get you anything?"

"Open it," he said.

When she opened the envelope, her eyes got huge.

"Juan, Juan, what are you doing?"

"Jada, will you marry me?"

All the people who saw what was happening hollered, "Say, Yes."

Tears started to flow, and in her tears, Juan heard a faint, "Yes, I will, Juan. You have made me so happy. I can honestly say that you surprised me. I never expected it."

Juan responded, "I love you. I did from the first time I met you. I'm just as happy."

She replied, "I'll wait until we get in the car before I give you a big kiss.

◆ ◆ ◆

Cindy traveled to the hospital after Conrad told her how serious the procedure was. The Neurosurgeon came out to see Conrad and Cindy before the surgery. The medical personnel still thought it was Parkinson's but wanted to ensure. He explained the procedure in detail and said the surgery should take about an hour. He was pleased it was caught early, so Rod's prognosis is excellent. He stated that with prompt and careful care, many people can recover and regain most, if not all, abilities they had before developing these symptoms.

This news caught Cindy and Conrad by surprise. Cindy pressed the surgeon, "You mean he may not have Parkinson's?"

The Neurosurgeon replied, "No, we think it is Parkinson's, but we want to eliminate other possibilities. Mr. Carson's symptoms point us to Parkinson's; however, some rare diseases or problems mimic Parkinson's. We shall soon find out. I'll come out when we're through."

Conrad responded, "Thank you, doctor, for that information."

With that said, the doctor turned and left. Cindy and Conrad took their seats in the waiting room. After checking her phone and looking for the time, she asked Conrad, "Why does waiting an hour in the hospital seem like five hours. And in a favorite clothing store, an hour seems like minutes?"

"Yeah, I feel the same in an auto parts store."

"Really?"

"Yes, when I see one thing I would like, it leads to another thing and another thing."

Cindy let that sink in for a moment, "You mean, guys can spend as much time in an auto parts store as a woman can spend in a clothing store?"

"I guess so," Conrad said as he scanned those well-worn magazines in waiting rooms.

They both got up from time to time because the chairs in the waiting room were not like the recliner chairs at home. They were rigid and inflexible.

Cindy was getting concerned until the surgeon entered the waiting room door and approached them.

"Everything went well. Rod is in ICU now for a couple of hours. We must keep monitoring him for that long before he can return to his room. Why don't you get something to eat. His vitals are all good."

"Thank you so much, doctor. We appreciate you telling us. When will we know what his prognosis is?"

"It may take a day or two. Don't worry. We will be in touch with Rod with the medical results."

The doctor turned to leave the waiting room.

Cindy looked at Conrad, "That's it? I don't know if I can wait a *couple of days*."

CHAPTER TWENTY-TWO

Two weeks later, there was pandemonium not only in San Jose but in Camarillo and Fresno, California. In Camarillo, last-minute changes and preparation for Aaron and Sue's wedding.

It was a fabulous sunny Thursday in all three locations.

In Southern California, Aaron's private secretary Ann was almost pulling her hair out because of all the last-minute details that needed to be done. She had to run to the church and ensure everything was ready for the rehearsal and wedding. Then Ann went off to the bakery to ensure the cake was ready. Then off to the Country Club to make last-minute arrangements for the rehearsal dinner and wedding luncheon. Finally, Ann could go to her hotel room and put her feet up.

After Juan's conversation with Jada about the marks on Al Fletcher's neck, Juan decided to do tests on the clothing Derik and Becky removed when they were brought into Fresno PD.

The tests came back to the Medical Examiner, and they were shocking. The M.E. came by Juan's office because she wanted to let him know personally.

She began with, "Derik is *not* the killer of Al Fletcher. The test on Becky Savage's shoelaces revealed the shoelaces were the weapon used to strangle him. She apparently shot him twice to make sure. Al Fletcher was killed by strangulation, and Becky Savage is the murderess."

Juan took another sip of his coffee, "Jada, the private detective I told you about from San Jose, told me it looked like shoe strings tied together. That's why I had their clothes tested, including their shoe laces. Jada was right."

After the M.E. left, Juan called Jada, "You're not going to believe what the tests came back as; who is the murderer?"

"No, who?"

"It wasn't Derik; it was Becky Savage. I've got to go. I will ask the patrol to pick her up and bring her in. Do you want to come and watch as I put the screws to her?"

"Sure do; I'll be right down. You want me to stop by and get some coffee for us?"

"Sure. See you soon, bye."

Juan really wanted to be the one to pick Becky up, but he knew the patrol guys would be faster.

Twenty minutes later, Juan received a call from patrol that Becky Savage was on her way into Homicide and the Interrogation Room. The patrol had already given Becky her rights. Becky called her lawyer, and he was on the way.

Juan and Jada watched Becky and her lawyer talk from a dark room next to the Interrogation Room. They could not hear because a lawyer is entitled to privacy when talking to a client. Juan left Jada in the room and went to his office to get a folder. He then came back and knocked on the Interrogation Room and entered. He sat across the table from them.

Juan started, "Becky, do you want to change anything about your story about what happened in Kings Canyon National Park?"

The lawyer spoke up, "What's going on here? Are you arresting my client?"

Juan paid the lawyer no attention, "What about it, Becky?"

The lawyer interrupted, "Don't say another word, Becky. This interview is over," as he started to leave.

"Sit down and shut up," Juan said to the lawyer.

Juan paused as the lawyer sat back down.

"Becky Savage, you are under arrest for the murder of Al Fletcher. I would advise you to do as your lawyer said. Keep quiet unless you want to tell me what happened up there."

The lawyer again advised her not to say anything. A female police officer entered the room and took her to another room to change into jail garb. The officer then took her to the Fresno jail.

Jada came out and went with Juan to his office.

"Thanks for letting me watch that. Almost like the movies."

"Not exactly; the movies or TV doesn't show all the tedious work before and after the arrest. The real work is just beginning. How about lunch?"

"Let's go. I'm hungry."

Since the surgery, Rod had not seen anyone in San Jose except Cindy and Conrad. The surgeon told him not to work and only stay home until he called. Staying home was very hard for a man who was used to being busy.

The call came in about one in the afternoon.

Cindy was with Rod when he answered the call,

"Hello?"

"This is Dr. Willow; we have good news. You do not have Parkinson's. The Spinal Tap and the Shunt procedure ruled it out. I won't get into the details of what the problem was until our follow-up in two weeks. I will be emailing you actions that you must follow to the letter. I am also writing you a couple of prescriptions for your pharmacy. I want you to get them today and take them as prescribed. Any Questions?"

"Just one, doctor. I'm supposed to take my secretary down the aisle for her wedding on Saturday in Southern California. Is it okay to go?"

"I would prefer you to fly instead of driving. I know you must be anxious about getting back to work. How about only three hours a day at the most. For now, I want you to do as little as possible. Don't drive yet until I give you the okay to drive. Anything else?"

"No doctor, and thank you so much. This is real news, good news. Bye."

"Well, well, *well*, what did he say?" Cindy said, getting very close to Rod.

Rod got emotional, and Cindy started to worry.

Finally, Rod wiped a tear from his eye.

"I **don't** have Parkinson's!"

Cindy then also cried. The tissue box was empty, so he had to get one from the other room. They both tried to compose themselves, but it was hard.

"That's wonderful, sweetheart. What *was* the problem?

"Apparently, not much. The doctor said he would give me the details when I attended the follow-up appointment in two weeks. We need to go to my pharmacy to pick up his prescribed medicine. He also said I will follow his email instructions to the letter."

On the way to the pharmacy, Rod called Aaron and told Aaron the news and told him not to tell Sue because he wanted to say it to her himself. He also told Aaron that he needed to fly there instead of driving. Aaron informed Rod that Aaron's personal Lear Jet would fly up there tomorrow morning to pick Rod up. The pilot would call him at the expected time of arrival.

Rod explained to Cindy what Aaron had said. Then Rod smiled, "How about we both take the jet down there. I need your company. I'll call Aaron back and tell him to get two rooms at the local hotel, okay?"

"That will save me from riding down there with Conrad. I would rather be with you anyway. I have things to tell you," Cindy said.

"What?"

"Not now, on the plane. The Plane – The Plane. Okay, it's from the old TV series Fantasy Island."

"I'm not that sick; I get it."

The following day at the San Jose office of Carson Detective Agency, everyone was back from the different cases around the region. Excitement was running high because Rod had an announcement to make. Cindy and Rod had their bags packed for a long extended weekend and maybe longer in Southern California. They arrived precisely at nine AM at the Carson office.

Everyone was in the large conference room. Refreshments were on the side tables, ready for the big meeting.

As Cindy and Rod entered the room, everyone stood and cheered. All he had told them was that it would be good news. They were so anxious to hear what it was. When they all had their drinks and goodies, they sat down and quieted down.

Rod stood before them. He became emotional, and his chin quivered. He looked around the room. Their support of him could not be measured or expressed. He looked at Conrad, who had been literally his right-hand man. He looked at the detectives that had labored so hard on their individual cases. He looked at his administration crew, who had worked long hours behind the scenes to accomplish their workload. He looked at Susan, who supported whatever he wanted or needed. He mouthed, **Thank You**, to each group. At last, he looks at Cindy. The tears began to flow.

Cindy came up and put her arms around his back, facing the employees.

"It's okay; take your time," Cindy said quietly.

After several moments, Rod took a drink of water.

Rod tried to talk, but the words would not come at first.

"I cannot express how I feel right now. You have stepped up to the plate and done your job excellently. If I pointed to one individual for their commitment to me and Carson's, I would offend the others who did outstanding work. I won't offend anyone here, but I would like you to know if you don't already know, that Conrad has gone way beyond what is expected of you as a friend and employee. Conrad, you have seen me at my worst this past month. Thank you, my friend."

Rod paused, "Now for the news. As you all know, I underwent a medical procedure to discover what I have been struggling with."

He paused again, "I do not have Parkinson's Disease."

A roar rose from the group as they stood and clapped. Rod held up his hands for quiet.

"I'm not finished. I do have a rare something that the Neurosurgeon said he would give me the details in our follow-up appointment. The doctor said that what he sees so far is that I will, if I do what they want, make a full recovery in a month or so. I mean with no effects of the access fluid in my head. If you want any gory details, see me when I return to work in a few weeks."

They again gave Rod a standing ovation.

After the meeting, Rod received a call from Aaron's pilot stating that he would touch down at eleven fifteen. Conrad would drive Rod and Cindy to the airport in San Jose.

Almost right on time, the sleek Bombardier Learjet Global 8000 arrived at a private hangar at the airport.

After the jet was fueled and ready, Rod and Cindy entered the private grand Learjet that seated eight people plus two crew seats and the pilot and co-pilot.

Rod and Cindy would have one crew member to accommodate their needs during the flight. Before the pilot started taxiing, the hostess asked if they wanted Champagne or wine. Rod looked at Cindy and said, "We'll take a glass of Champagne, please."

"I'll get that for you as soon as we level off at our flight altitude."

They buckled in as the jet got to the main runway. It was a smooth takeoff and a steady climb to around forty thousand feet. Soon Rod and Cindy had their drinks and were chatting up a storm.

Rod said, "Okay, you wanted to tell me something. What did I do now?"

"Nothing silly. I wanted to talk to you about Cory."

"Cory, who?"

"Oh, come on, you know, the guy I had a couple of dates with?"

"That guy."

"Yes, that guy. When he called for the second date, I went to my favorite spot in my bedroom by the window. I wrote down my thoughts. What I wanted in my life? Where I saw myself in ten years? And who I wanted to be with for the rest of my life. It's surprising how clear it becomes when someone takes the time to examine and write down your thoughts. It soon became very clear about my decision."

Cindy paused to take another sip of Champagne. She continued, "I decided to let Cory pick me up because I wanted to tell him about my feelings in person. Rod, I love you with all my heart."

Rod whispered, "And I love you, also."

"Cory was a true gentleman. After I told him that I was through dating anyone but you, he said he understood and thought this relationship would not go anywhere. He took me home, and like a gentleman, he escorted me to the door. He kissed me on the cheek, smiled, turned, returned to his car, and drove away."

Tears were flowing down her cheeks before she finished talking. She went to the restroom to freshen up and returned with all smiles. They hugged and kissed.

Rod said, "Thank you for your honesty. I thought you might have had a close encounter with yourself because, since that time, you have been a different person."

"How was I different?"

"A lot more mature, settled, down to earth, and happy with yourself. You know, growing up to a full-fledged woman."

Cindy smiled and squeezed his hand, "Yes, I agree with you. I do feel different. I'm glad it shows."

"Cindy, I think it's time we get engaged."

"What? Now, that's romantic. Where's the ring?"

Before Aaron and Sue's wedding rehearsal, Rod took Sue aside to give her the news. Sue cried and said, "I'm sure glad you didn't wait until tomorrow when we walked down the aisle. Rod, I am so happy for you. Now let's get the rehearsal done so we can eat."

The rehearsal went smoothly, and the dinner afterward was scrumptious. Rod and Cindy, Conrad, Aaron and Sue, Ann and the rest of the wedding party had a great time. Conrad was the life of the party. He had some pre-wedding jokes that had everyone in stitches all night. He said he had many more fun things to discuss at the wedding luncheon.

Rod, Cindy, and Conrad went to breakfast Saturday morning. Conrad was still in a great mood and in high spirits. Conrad didn't know that Cindy was flashing a colossal engagement diamond, and Conrad never took the hint.

Finally, Cindy shoved her hand within inches of his eyes,

"Conrad, are you that clueless?"

Conrad took a hard, long look at Cindy's left hand.

It was beginning to register when he looked at both of them, "Are you guys engaged? That was a dumb question, wasn't it?"

"Yes, we are, Conrad," Rod said, laughing.

"When did this happen? I guess I am clueless."

Cindy and Rod laughed, then Cindy responded, "Yesterday, on the plane coming down here."

Conrad was still shocked. "How did it happen, Cindy?"

"Well, I'll say this." Rod was laughing in the background.

"It was about as romantic as watching a boxing match. Rod said, 'Cindy, I think it's time we get engaged.' Can you believe it?"

"Rod, you rascal, even I could do better than that?"

Rod responded, embarrassed, "I guess I could have made a bigger deal out of it."

Cindy asked Rod, "You could have made a bigger deal out of it?"

Rod was very embarrassed now, "Forget it. Let's talk about something else. You both know I've been sick lately."

Conrad had to respond, "Oh, we're going to use that excuse now? Knowing you, you'll use that for a long time."

The wedding was spectacular. Everything went well. When Aaron saw Sue coming down the aisle, he kept smiling through the rest of the service. The ground floor of the church was filled with family and friends.

Then Aaron saw his son, William, sitting in the row with other family members. William was with another man; he did not know. Aaron whispered something to the preacher and Sue, then walked over to his son, William, and hugged him. They remained there for a moment longer. Aaron whispered something to William, returning to the stage with a giant smile.

The rest of the service was *average*.

During the reception, Conrad was like an old pro with a microphone. His delivery was flawless. At times people were laughing, and at other times, many had to wipe tears from their eyes. The clicking of forks against glasses could be heard all night long. The dancing had almost everyone on the dance floor except for the first one with Aaron and Sue.

After things began to wind down, Rod went to Aaron.

"Aaron, what are the plans for the honeymoon?"

"Don't tell anyone yet, but I'm taking her to Fiji Islands. She doesn't also know that on another plane I charted, I am taking her mom and Sue's two children there also."

"Wow, Aaron, you are quite a man. That's fantastic. I wish I could be there to see her face. Aaron, dear friend, have a wonderful time and life with Sue. She deserves it."

"Thanks; when I saw you and Sue coming down the aisle, I almost lost it. When I saw William, you know."

"Yes, and how did he get out of prison, and who was that other guy that stayed very close to him?"

"Oh, the guy with him was a Marshall who transported him from prison. James pulled some heavy strings to allow William to attend our wedding."

Rod said, "Cindy and I will visit a Santa Barbara resort for a week. Conrad is also coming to keep me in line."

CHAPTER TWENTY-THREE

Aaron and Sue had to stop in Hawaii to refuel, so they decided to go to the harbor and see the WWII sunken ship, the Arizona. It was still leaking some oil which the legend says was tears from the ship.

After an hour at the Arizona Memorial, Aaron told Sue they had to go because lunch was ready on the plane.

The hostess soon had lunch for them when they reached cruising altitude.

Sue was doing some thinking as they ate. *God, you have been so good to me. Help me to be the kind of wife that Aaron needs.*

Aaron was sitting quietly. He had his eyes on his new wife. He could tell she was pondering.

Aaron finally said, "You're deep in thought, is something wrong?"

"Oh, no. On the contrary. I want to be the best wife ever. Help me to know how to please and comfort you."

Aaron turned and looked into her eyes, "You have already made me a delighted man. I want to tell you something.

"I've been thinking about this for a few months. I want to retire and let others build up the company. James is coming back to work. He'll be working with our CEO, Dennis Gilbert. James has a vast knowledge of Sterling and has grown up a lot. What do you think of that?"

Sue thought momentarily, "If that's what you want to do? What will I do with a man around the house all day?"

Aaron stopped eating, "I've got some golfing and fishing to do. I can't stay around the house all day with you."

They both laughed. Sue was beginning to understand what the future holds for both of them. They continued to talk, laugh, cry, and talk some more. Sue was getting tired, so she laid her head on his shoulder.

Sus woke up with the pilot announcing it would be twenty minutes before they would land in Fiji.

"Aaron, I am so looking forward to our time alone here. I hope mom and the kids are okay back in California?"

Aaron only smiled.

After the check-in and luggage retrieval, they went outside.

The expression on Sue's face when she saw her mom was priceless. But when her children jumped out to surprise her, she was overwhelmed. She ran to them and gave them long hugs. She turned to Aaron with the sweetest expression, "Aaron, you are something else. Who would consider bringing my mom and my children to this faraway paradise."

Aaron responded, "They're not here to be with us all the time; we have a honeymoon to celebrate. Most of the time, they will be busy with their own activities. You see, I brought two sitters so your mom can enjoy Fiji."

Sue was flabbergasted by the dimension of Aaron's ability to make everything perfect. She wanted to express herself, but the words never came out.

Aaron said, "That's okay; you don't have to say anything."

Aaron then approached Mrs. Stillard, "You have a great time here. Do whatever you want to because it's all on me. Here's a credit card. Go, have fun."

Turning back to Sue, "Mrs. Sterling, are you ready for an adventure of your lifetime?"

Aaron had pre-rented a Jeep Grand Cherokee for their time on the main island. Soon they were on their way to the Honeymoon Cottage Aaron had arraigned while in Fiji. They decided to rest and have dinner there before exploring the following day.

Aaron and Sue dived into a lagoon's gorgeous reef on Fiji's southern coast. Shark diving was out of the question, so they enjoyed the reef more. With fantastic mountains and championship golf courses, they traveled the island in the Jeep with no cover over their heads. It wasn't long before their hair flowed, and they had rosy cheeks.

Aaron and Sue enjoyed a few days on overwater resort cottages with all the amenities you could ever ask for.

They were basking in the sun on lounge chairs when Sue asked Aaron, "Can't we stay here forever? I don't want this time to end. Aaron, you have made me a thrilled woman."

Aaron responded, "Sue, I also wish that we could stay, but even good things must come to an end. We still have a few more days, so let's enjoy every moment."

They joined other vacationers in a jet boat going up the famous Navua River. The canopy of sharp cliffs and waterfalls along the shoreline gave them spectacular views, and they enjoyed invigorating rapids.

With Aaron's plane, they explored different islands in

Fiji. One of the more remote islands had no airport, so they took a boat to take in the natural and cultural experiences.

On the last night in Fiji, Aaron brought a meal and drinks to their hotel suite. They were tired but delighted to bring their fantastic honeymoon to an end.

After they blessed their food, Aaron looked intently at Sue, "You have made me the happiest man on earth. I had a great first marriage, but now I know I've never been more satisfied. I'm looking forward to many years with you."

Sue said, "I'm also thrilled you chose me."

That night in bed, Sue turned to Aaron. She threw her arms around him, "Honey, this has been the most wonderful time I have ever had. It was also good to have Mom and *our* children here also. We managed to have just the right amount of time with them. Not too much, not too little. Thank you, I love you."

The following day was early rising for the Sterlings.

Aaron's plane was soon on the way for the long trip back to Hawaii. They spent the night in Honolulu before heading back to the Mainland.

Both Aaron and Sue wondered what the future held for them. Time will tell. *Time will tell.*

a time of mourning for their son Roger. The pain of losing one of their children was sometimes overwhelming. Roger's mother, Dawn, seemed to take it the hardest. Everyone saw Dawn's expression of pain, but Joe's was inward. It took him longer to process Roger's death and how he died.

The casket was kept closed because of obvious reasons.

The family had to keep their memories of Roger from the past, not what they would have seen in the coffin.

Roger's sister helped her parents by giving a beautiful tribute to her brother at the funeral. Because the Brooks family was well known in the community, there were a lot of people that came to give their condolences.

Joe, Dawn, Angel, and her husband went to their mountain cabin after the funeral to try to rebound. Joe loved the mountains because he and Roger had spent many days at their cabin doing lots of hiking and fishing.

Joe found solace in the giant trees around their home away from home. After the third day, Dawn found Joe down by the water.

"Joe, how are you doing?"

"Better; I love this area so much. Peaceful, restful, and healing. I can't believe how bad I took Roger's death. I keep my feelings inward, and I know that is totally wrong. Out here, I'm able to talk to God. I've yelled at God. How could this happen to people like us? I told God it's not fair."

Dawn didn't respond; she just listened.

Joe continued, "That sounds silly now, but I had to get it out of my system or go crazy. God quietly reminded me that He is still in control. I mean everything. Even something as tragic as Roger's death. Rod's detectives told me that Roger only had fun and saw new things. Just a slip, a fall; I wish I could have been there. Roger was struggling with some things but sent us a message."

"What do you mean? He sent us a message?"

Joe said with tears, "I don't think I told you. After he fell, he wrote on the ground. *Love you, Mom and d....*, He didn't finish writing the word *dad*."

Dawn started crying, "No, you didn't tell me. That's

okay. I don't think I could have taken it before now. Thank you for sharing that with me."

Joe slowly got to his feet, "We didn't hear him express love too much. But with his last breath, he expressed what was inside him. I'm grateful that he wrote that."

Joe and Dawn slowly climbed the stairs to the cabin through the trees and bushes.

They were ready to start a new chapter of life.

A party was at one of Carson's detectives, David Turner's home. David had a big house with a vast backyard, many trees, and landscaped grass and plants.

All of Carson's personnel were enjoying some time off.

David, Josh, Marcus, Javier, and Jada were back from Fresno, California. Susan brought Jordan and Victoria, who completed the staff except for Conrad, Rod, and Cindy.

Jerry and Eva came also bringing more refreshments.

David had set up a large circle of chairs around the outdoor fire pit. He asked staff to bring different food and drinks that would be enough for a small army. David also brought fixings for smores and large fluffy marshmallows.

Jada, Marcus, and Javier were the cutups for the night. They all laughed, and soon, stories of their escapades were getting lots of laughs.

David told a tall tale, "My dad told me this story when he was a kid. They went to a church camp, and one scary night, this older youth pastor in the cabin said the kids needed to go hunting. He told them to get their top sheets and flashlights and accompany him.

Soon the kids were out in the woods, and the pastor

kept looking up at the trees until he found a nice group of trees. He told them to find a big heavy limb they could carry. He explained that the kids needed to place their sheets around the tree's base. Then he told those with the limbs they could start beating on the trees. The Snipes would run down the tree into their sheets if they hit hard enough. They would then fold up the sheets to capture the Snipes.

By this time, David had the group rolling on the ground. A few didn't get it.

David went on. The kids pounded and pounded, but nothing came down from the trees. The youth pastor told them they might not have hit hard enough, or it wasn't Snipe season.

Jada asked, "What's a Snipe?"

The group really started laughing.

At David's party, things were winding down. David stood and raised his hands to quiet the group.

"Before you start, David, I have an announcement," Jada stood and said, "If you look at my left hand, you will see a ginormous ring. I'm engaged to the Head Detective of the Fresno Police Department."

The group erupted in applause, and the girls ran over to see the ring and give Jada hugs.

Jada said, "No date yet, but you all will know first. I promise."

When the chattering stopped, David said, "I have an idea. I don't know about you all, but we should pool our money and get Rod and Cindy a nice gift. You know, from the staff. We have seen a true miracle with Rod's new diagnosis and their recent engagement."

Some were surprised by David saying they were engaged. Soon they all dug deep to give money to Rod and Cindy as the hat went around the group.

David then raised his hands again, "Maybe some of you were not prepared, so we'll have the hat in the break room at work so you can give it there. I want to thank you for coming and making this a memorable night. You can stay as long as you want. We have plenty of food and drinks. If you are more energetic, maybe some of you could go Snipe hunting."

CHAPTER TWENTY-FOUR

After a hectic couple of months, Rod and Cindy let down their hair and adored a fabulous week at the Rosewood Miramar Beach Resort in Santa Barbara, California. The summer was winding down, and the weather was as stunning as the surroundings.

Conrad was nowhere to be seen except when he joined them at breakfast and an occasional dinner when invited. Cindy and Rod stayed at the beach for the first few days, enjoying the white sand and surf. They laid on some super big beach towels and talked for hours and hours. Sometimes, they only sat back and took in the sun.

Rod was feeling much better, and the sun seemed the best medicine. The concerns of his health and business woes drifted away with each sound of the surf coming into the beach. Giving Sue away at the wedding was an extraordinary emotional luxury, especially for a single guy. Aaron and Sue were so happy, and Rod could only imagine Sue's reaction when she saw her mom and her children in the Fiji Islands. Rod's engagement with Cindy brought fire to his bones, and he felt like a new man.

Cindy would, most of the time at the beach, turn and look at the passion of her life. She was ecstatic because she had become a woman in love. She dreamed of their time together, starting a family and growing old with each other. They had yet to talk about the wedding date. She only wanted to spend as much time as possible with him.

The week was perfect as far as the weather was concerned. It sprinkled a little, but nothing to dampen their spirits. Walking on the surf without shoes always took the worries of life away.

Thursday, they spent the afternoon on the resort's outdoor patio. With drinks on their table, the conversation finally got to set a date for their wedding.

Cindy could not stop smiling, "I don't want our wedding in a hurry, but not too long either. What are you thinking?"

Rod stretched, "Do you want a spring wedding, a June wedding, or a fall wedding?"

When a waitress came and asked if they wanted another drink, Cindy was deep in thought.

"Sure, how about you, hon?"

"Yes, how about champagne this time?"

"Oh, yes, that sounds good," Cindy told Rod and the waitress.

Cindy then looked back to Rod, "Everyone does June weddings. I don't know about spring weddings. How about a fall wedding? They have so many beautiful places around Napa Valley to choose from. Let's plan a fall wedding for, let's see, October. What do you think?

"I've always loved the fall. Yes, let's do it. This fall."

Cindy laughed, "No, you don't. Next year in October. When I return home, I'll check with the folks about a good date. You know, Dad has things lined up years in advance. We'll talk to them together. Mom will try to control things, so I know I must put my foot down."

They both laughed. Rod also knew it was true. A few moments later, Cindy said, "Rod, do you think Conrad likes Susan? I hope so; I really like her."

"It's hard to tell. At times he is really private. He said a couple of weeks ago that he was thinking about marriage."

Cindy responded, "Maybe, We can...." Rod quickly answered, "No, you don't; we are not matchmakers. Let us let Conrad drive his own car. He's proficient."

"You're too funny," Cindy said as she gave Rod a punch.

Conrad left the resort on Friday, and Rod and Cindy would stay until Saturday morning after breakfast.

As they got into the rental car. Cindy turned to Rod.

"Rod, I love you more today than I did yesterday. I pray that our love will grow and grow until we get old together."

Rod could only nod yes, as he stretched over and deposited an exceptionally long-lasting kiss.

Cindy reached over, squeezed his hand, and said, "Now that is settled, let's talk about Conrad and Susan."

The End

ABOUT *THE AUTHOR*

R Curtis Ford was born in Detroit, Michigan, spent his young years in Western Michigan, and now resides in Chaska, Minnesota. He and his wife, Ann, now in Memory Care, have three children. Family life has always centered around our faith. After his time in the U.S. Air Force, he went to a Bible College for music and worked at several churches as Youth and Young Adults Minister and Music Minister. R Curtis Ford retired from the Department of Defense as a Police Officer, Training Officer, Weapons Range Director, and Emergency Management Officer for two Naval Bases in Southern California. This experience was the backdrop for his first book, *Deadly Roads*. *Deadly Trails* is his second book in the series, Mysteries of a Detective #2

Made in the USA
Monee, IL
19 January 2024

52052661R00132